The T“telepl

James Pattinson

Table of Contents

Chapter One – Hogan

"IS that Mr Rowan?" the voice on the telephone said. "Mr Charles Rowan?"

It was a man's voice and Rowan did not recognise it. There was no clearly regional accent about it; it was neutral, a trifle coarse perhaps, not loud, rather low-pitched, almost, one might have said, confidential in tone.

"Yes."

"I've been meaning to have a word with you, Mr Rowan. It's about that last book of yours — *Dead Come Morning*. It's good. Best you've done, I'd say."

"So you've read others of mine?"

"Oh, sure. Just about all of them. Fact is, you're my favourite author."

"Well, that's nice to know."

"Don't mind me giving you a call?"

"Why, no," Rowan said. "It's always a pleasure to hear from a satisfied reader. I'm glad you enjoyed the book."

"Enjoyed it, yes. Clever. Very ingenious. Well written too. I like a book to be well written."

Rowan felt a glow of satisfaction. What writer could fail to be gratified at having his work praised? The glow lasted for perhaps ten seconds. Then the man said:

"But you could do better."

The glow faded immediately. This sounded too much like criticism, and that was a very different kettle of fish. Rowan was annoyed; it was doubtful whether any author, alive or dead, had ever accepted criticism, from whatever quarter it might have come, without at least a trace of resentment. And this unknown caller on the telephone: what qualification did he have for passing judgement on a book written by someone of the standing of Charles Rowan? The phrase, 'could do better', was reminiscent of a school report; and who the devil was this person who had the audacity to trot it out right here and now? It was damned cheek; it certainly was.

"I can help you," the man said, "if you'll let me."

Rowan suppressed a groan. He could guess what was coming: the fellow had a plot for a novel. Sometimes it seemed to him that half the people in the country had a plot for a novel and were just looking for someone else to do the purely hack-work of filling it out and writing it down. Some of them were quite tenacious and took a deal of choking off; they seemed to be unable to understand why you were not ready to jump at the chance of taking up what was being offered.

He should have put a stop to it right there; it might have saved him a cartload of trouble if he had. But maybe just slamming the receiver down would not have been enough; the man would almost certainly have rung again. Someone like this, someone with a purpose, with a crazy idea in the head, an *idée fixe* as the term was, would not have been so easily put off.

"If you're offering me a plot," Rowan said, "you're wasting your time and mine. I don't want it."

"Don't be so sure of that. This wouldn't be any ordinary crime novel plot; it'd be the real thing."

"I don't get it. Anyway, who are you?"

"You can call me Hogan."

"Is that a Christian name or a surname?"

"Never mind which. And you asked the wrong question. You should have asked not who but what I am."

"Okay. So what are you?"

"I am a murderer," the man said.

So he was a joker. Rowan was even more annoyed, and he made no attempt to disguise the annoyance in his voice. "Look," he said, "I'm in no mood for fooling. And you really are wasting my time. Do you think I've got nothing better to do than listen to your nonsense?"

But he did not ring off. Somehow, he could not do it. He had to hear what more Hogan had to say.

"It's not nonsense, Mr Rowan. And I think you know it's not." Hogan was still speaking in that quiet confidential manner he had used from the start. "In your heart you know it, don't you?"

"I know nothing of the sort," Rowan said. Nothing except that he was talking to a nut-case and ought to terminate the conversation by hanging up on this man who called himself Hogan. "You're crazy."

A faint chuckle came over the line. Hogan sounded amused. "Is that what you think?"

"What else am I to think?"

"But you're still listening. That means you're interested. It means you can't be sure I'm not telling the truth. Am I right?"

Rowan said nothing.

"So you're not going to admit it. No matter. Makes no difference. You'll want evidence, of course. Stands to reason. Can't be expected just to take my word for it. Well, I can give you proof."

"What kind of proof?"

"The best of all. The body of the victim."

"You're going to bring it here for me to see?" Rowan spoke with heavy sarcasm.

"Now you're the one that's joking," Hogan said. "That really would be crazy, wouldn't it?"

"Then what are you going to do?"

"I'm going to give you a clue."

"What clue?"

"The Lazar House," Hogan said.

He rang off. Rowan could hear the rattling sound before the line went dead. Hogan had said his piece and brought the conversation to a close on his terms.

Rowan put down the receiver and did some thinking. He knew where the Lazar House was. It was an old ruin of a flint and brick building that in the distant past had been used for the accommodation of lepers well away from the nearest town. Or so the story went. But it had been abandoned long ago. It was in an isolated position with no other building near it, and the ground all round it was in a neglected state; trees and scrub having been allowed to grow as they would, with little if any attempt to keep them under control. It was as if the memory of what it had been used for in the past was enough to make it shunned even today.

Rowan's cottage was itself somewhat removed from any neighbours, although a drive of three miles or so along a minor country road would bring him to a sizable market town which could boast a supermarket or two amongst its other amenities. The name of the town was Wingstead, and it was there that Rowan went for the necessities of life. Rather nearer in the opposite direction was a village called Little Madding which had once had two shops, three public houses and a post-office, but now had none of these. Half the properties seemed to have been bought as second homes by well-to-do Londoners who used them mostly at weekends and took no real part in the life of the community. As a nucleus of rural culture Little

Madding, like many other villages, might have been said to be dying if not already dead.

Charles Rowan had bought his cottage, not as a weekend retreat but as a home where he could write in peace, undistracted by the rush and bustle of the great city; and after a couple of years he was still enchanted with it. There was of course much that was still beguiling about London. Most of his friends were there, and there were parties and entertainments which were a great attraction. But it was little more than an hour's drive up to town and he would often spend a few days there as a break from his labours on the latest book. It was in fact during one of these breaks that Julia appeared on the scene; and this complicated matters somewhat.

It happened at a party given by Paul and Mary Stanton. The Stantons were much the same age as Rowan, thirtyish. Paul was in advertising and doing pretty well. They were both fond of company and were forever inviting people to their house in Maida Vale for drinks and maybe a meal. You met all sorts there; Paul and Mary had a wide circle of acquaintances and believed in keeping in touch.

Julia Spence was a brunette and had a lot going for her physically. Rowan was attracted at once. For the rest of the evening he was never far from her side, and she appeared to be quite happy with the arrangement. He discovered that she was an artist with a house and studio in the Highgate area of North London. She told him that she had read a couple of his books and enjoyed them; which would have been enough to persuade him to look upon her with favour even if there had not been all the other attributes drawing him to her.

"I hope," he said, "you're not saying that just to please me."

"Why should I want to please you?"

"That's a good question. You could, of course, simply have been being polite."

"That's true. And then you could have reciprocated by saying how much you admired my paintings."

"I should have been delighted to do so, but for one snag."

"And that is?"

"I've never seen any of them."

"And until tonight you'd never even heard of me?"

Reluctantly he had to admit that he had not. "Should I?"

She smiled. "I'd have been rather surprised if you had. Gratified of course, but surprised nonetheless. I'm not famous. Yet."

"But you hope to be?"

"We all have our dreams," she said. "What would life be without them?"

"I should like to see some of your work," Rowan said.

"Really?"

"Yes, really."

"You're not just being polite now?"

"Not at all." It was the truth. It was not so much that he was interested in her painting, which might be terrible, but that he was very much interested in her.

"Well," she said, "I see no reason why it could not be arranged if it's really what you'd like."

"Oh, it is."

*

In the event he did not have to make any pretence of appreciation when he went out to her place for a private viewing of her latest work: the canvases that had not yet been sold or put on show. He had been afraid she might have been one of those ultra-modern artists who just threw blobs of paint around or made squares and circles and rectangles like exercises in coloured geometry; but she was obviously not a member of either of these schools. Yet it was not chocolate box art either. London figured in a lot of the paintings: the City, the river, the parks, the Tower, Saint Paul's . . . all done with a kind of impressionistic effect which he found particularly attractive.

"But these are wonderful," he said.

"You don't need to sound so amazed. What were you expecting? Something dreadful?"

"I didn't know what to expect."

"Of course you didn't, but you thought you might have to put on a show of liking what you really thought was pretty ghastly stuff. Isn't that so?"

"Well —"

"Oh," she said, "you don't have to deny it."

"Then I won't."

"But now you've seen it and you think it's not so bad after all?"

"I think it's great."

"I hope you're not saying that just to please me."

He laughed. She was repeating with a touch of mockery the words he himself had used on the occasion of their first meeting. "You can be sure of that," he said. "I am being perfectly honest."

"Yes," she said, after treating him to a particularly searching look, "I believe you are."

"Not of course that I wouldn't do anything to please you."

This made her laugh too, and he liked the sound of her laughter. "May I have that in writing?"

"If you will provide the pen and the paper."

*

It was so obvious to both of them that they were made for each other that it scarcely needed any discussion. Mary Stanton was delighted.

"I knew it. I just knew it would be like this. I'm so glad I introduced you."

"We're glad too," Julia said. "Aren't we, Charles?"

"No doubt about it," Rowan said. "It was the best thing that could have happened."

But there were drawbacks. Rowan had his cottage deep in the East Anglian countryside and Julia had her studio in Highgate, a matter of sixty or more miles separating the two. For a time things worked well enough. He would drive up to London and spend a few days at Julia's place and she would reciprocate by driving down to Flint Cottage for an equivalent stay with him. But this kind of arrangement played havoc with their work schedules and they both realised that something needed to be done about it.

To Rowan the solution appeared obvious. "Why don't you give up your Highgate house and come and live at the cottage? There'd be plenty of room."

That was true: it had once been a pair of cottages but had been made into one by the former owner. It would not have been difficult to convert some of the space into a studio. Besides which, the surrounding countryside would provide a host of subjects for the artist's brush.

But Julia rejected the suggestion out of hand. For her London was indispensable as the base for operations; it was the very heart of her world, the centre of everything. To move out to the backwoods as Rowan had done would be a disaster.

"My inspiration is here, don't you see? This is where all the action is. The cottage is all very well now and then as a place to relax in, but as a permanency it's simply not on. A far better plan would be for you to sell it and move in here with me. After all, you can write anywhere, can't you?"

He could see that from her point of view this appeared perfectly logical, and had he not himself discovered that living in the country was not without its snags? So why not do as Julia had suggested? Would it not be the reasonable course to take? Yet, perversely perhaps, now that the possibility of giving up the cottage and returning to London had been suggested to him he found himself curiously reluctant to do so. There was much that he liked about the place after all; and, besides, was the Highgate house really large enough to accommodate an artist and an author on a permanent basis? Would they not be forever getting in each other's way? And by moving in with her he would be losing much of his independence; there could be no doubt about that. The place would not be his and he could foresee all kinds of problems arising. One had to be clear-sighted about such matters and not rush blindly into an arrangement that one might live to regret.

Which did not mean that he loved Julia any the less; it was simply a question of taking the long view and working out what would really be best for both of them. Unfortunately, in this matter what would be best for both of them was something on which they could not see eye to eye.

So the situation remained as it was; the problem was unresolved. He continued to drive up to London and she to make the journey down into the country. They agreed that it was an unsatisfactory state of affairs, but they could not agree on a way of changing it for the better.

*

And now, as if he had not already enough to distract him from his writing, there was this man who called himself Hogan ringing up with his crazy talk of a murder that he had committed. It was all nonsense, of course; the man was undoubtedly a crank or a practical joker. The best course would be simply to put it out of his mind and get down to work, to the job of putting on paper the words and sentences that earned him a living.

He decided to do just that. Unfortunately, however, it was not so easily done. He could not get the thought of Hogan out of his mind; it remained there, nagging at him. What kind of a man was he? What did he look like? There was no way of telling; he had nothing to go on except the sound of a voice on the telephone; and this could have been disguised.

He tried to picture a face that would match the voice; but of course it was a futile exercise and nothing came of it. He wondered why the man should have chosen him to make his confession to. If it was a confession. But of course he had given the reason, had he not? Or at least he had given a reason. It was because he had read one of Rowan's books. No, not one,

11

nearly all of them; that was what he had said. Up to that point it had all been plain sailing: a grateful reader praising the work of his favourite author; flattering him; boosting his ego. And all would have been fine if he had not spoiled things by adding a few ill-chosen words: "But you could do better". That was where it all began to go wrong; from then on it became steadily worse; it became really crazy.

Yet the man had not sounded crazed. He had spoken calmly, lucidly, never raising his voice, giving no indication of any excitement, of being in the least degree demented. And if he had been a hoaxer would he not have made some attempt to give the impression of being under a certain amount of mental stress? Would this not have been a part of the act? Perhaps. And again, perhaps not. Who could tell?

Rowan made another attempt to banish the matter from his mind and get started again at the point where he had been interrupted by the ringing of the telephone. But it was no use; he was not making sense in the words that he put down; Hogan persisted in coming between him and the story he was concocting, confusing him, making it impossible to go on.

"Damn him!" Rowan muttered. "Damn the man!"

But damning him was not going to mend things. He pushed back the chair from his desk and stood up. He had to face the fact: there was only one way of getting rid of the baneful influence of Hogan, and that was by going to the Lazar House and taking a look inside. It was stupid; he would find nothing and he was a fool to allow himself to be pushed into this action by a nutter; but stupid or not, he had to do it, because until he had he could not write another word.

Inwardly fuming at being forced to do so against his will, he pulled on a zipper jacket, picked up his car keys and let himself out of the cottage.

Chapter Two – The Real Thing

THE Lazar House was less than a mile from Flint Cottage, down a narrow byway known as Low Lane which branched off the road to Wingstead and meandered snakelike to nowhere in particular. It took Rowan only few minutes to reach it in the red Ford Mondeo which he had only recently bought to replace an ageing Vauxhall, and he parked the car on the wide verge where, in this latter end of summer, there remained a rich variety of fading wild flowers laced with brambles and creepers.

The house was hardly visible from the lane, being almost hidden by the untended wood that had grown up around it. There had at one time in the past been a wooden fence and a gate marking the boundary of the property, but these had rotted into near extinction, and what had once been a short driveway was now practically indistinguishable from its surroundings.

Some thirty yards further down the lane was an ancient hump-backed bridge with brick arches spanning a shallow stream which trickled through the wood and widened out into some marshy ground on the other side. The lane was little used by traffic, and when he got out of his car Rowan was struck by the air of remoteness of this spot, although it was not so very far from a town and a small village. Deserted as it was at this moment, it could have been miles from anywhere, and as soon as he had left the road and ventured past the last remains of the rotted gate he experienced a sense of having trespassed on some forbidden territory where he had no right to be.

It was a warm day, though overcast, and there seemed to be a threat of thunder. Under the trees the atmosphere was oppressive; it was as though there were a lack of oxygen, and the rampant undergrowth made it necessary for him to pick his way with care. He wondered who the property belonged to; possibly it was part of a large estate or farm; but whoever the owner was, it was apparent that he treated this particular area with complete neglect, possibly leaving it deliberately to nature as a sanctuary for wild life where birds and animals could exist relatively undisturbed.

The house was larger than he had expected. He had never previously been close up to it, and the glimpse that he had caught on a few occasions when passing in the lane had given little evidence of the considerable size of the building. There were outhouses attached to it, arranged so as to form two sides of a courtyard at the rear, and ivy had grown up the walls and even spread to the roof. There was not a single unbroken pane of glass remaining in any of the windows, which were like sightless eyes staring blindly at the surrounding trees.

Rowan walked all round the house and outbuildings before venturing inside. Though he did not admit as much to himself, he felt a certain reluctance to go into that old decaying pile where according to legend so many miserable lepers had ended their days. If any house deserved to be haunted surely this one did. But haunting was nonsense, and he had not come there to search for a ghost but something altogether more substantial, though perhaps no less horrifying to behold.

Yet of course there would be nothing, ghostly or material; he was convinced of that and was there simply for the purpose of lending incontrovertible proof to this conviction. So why was he hanging around outside when the obvious thing to do was to go in and search the place? Why not get the matter over and done with, so that he could go back to the cottage and get on with the work that this fellow Hogan had interrupted?

"Okay," he muttered, answering his own unspoken question. "Okay, I'll do it. Don't rush me."

He walked to the front door — or rather the doorway — since the door itself had disappeared; maybe taken away by someone who had an alternative use for it. The frame was still there; it was of heavy oak and had stood the test of time, protected as it was by a stone porch that was practically indestructible. Inside he came to what had been no doubt the entrance hall; it was bare now, the floor strewn with fallen plaster, the walls damp and mildewed.

There was an odour of putrefaction and decay which he found highly repellent. He felt a disinclination to proceed further into the building, but it would have been an admission of timidity to have retreated now, and stupid as well; having come so far he had to make a thorough search of the place, improbable though it might be that he would discover anything of interest. So, conquering his unwillingness to do so, he began methodically to go from room to room, stepping gingerly over the rubbish littering the floors and unimpeded by any surviving door. The house was a honeycomb of passageways and chambers of various shapes and sizes, all eerily silent, all with that dank oppressive smell which he found so offensive to the nostrils.

Any temptation he might have had to explore the upper floors would have been immediately dismissed by an inspection of what remained of the staircases. These worm-eaten ruins were not in any condition to bear the weight of a man, and if Hogan had in fact ever been in this ancient ruin of a house, which was a matter for doubt, he would most certainly never have ventured higher than the ground floor. Rowan, therefore, had no difficulty in deciding to confine his search to the lower rooms, peering into every nook and corner of the decaying pile and aided only by the rather dim light that filtered in through the ivy-festooned windows.

And he found nothing. Hogan had been gulling him; he became more and more convinced of this the further he progressed. He had been sent on a fool's errand and he should have had the good sense not to fall for such an obvious hoax. Annoyed with himself, convinced now that he was simply wasting his time, he nevertheless continued the search, determined to see it through to the end, futile though it might be.

He came finally to what appeared to have been a kitchen. There was a stone sink and the rusted remains of a pump, and through a doorway could be seen the courtyard at the back of the house where weeds had grown up between the flagstones, and even a few elders and thorns had taken root in patches of bare earth.

Rowan gazed all round this large room. Years ago the walls would have been whitewashed; now they were a dingy grey in colour. This presumably was where food for the lepers had been prepared; he wondered idly what it had been; pretty wretched stuff probably. They would not have been fed on the fat of the land. It was likely that the bread had been baked there; indeed, there was a brick oven at one end of the kitchen, the iron door still intact.

As soon as he noticed this door he saw that an arrow had been marked on the wall just above it, pointing downward. He walked across to the oven, and as he drew nearer he could see that the arrow had surely been put there recently, possibly gouged into the plaster with a large nail or something of that description. At once the reason why the mark had been made became evident to him; it was pointing directly at the oven door and could only indicate that the door should be opened, that something was concealed within the oven.

15

Rowan experienced an intense reluctance to proceed any further. If it was indeed Hogan who had made the mark — and this now seemed only too probable — was it not also probable that the oven contained something unpleasantly gruesome? Something he had no desire to see. He felt a powerful urge to beat a hasty retreat, to leave that gloomy oppressive building and go back to his car and drive away. He regretted that he had come to the house, had allowed himself to be persuaded by that insinuating voice on the telephone. He should have ignored it; he was certain of that now; but still he could not quite bring himself to abandon the search at this late stage. Curiosity alone would have been enough to spur him on to a conclusion. He had to discover what, if anything, was concealed within the oven.

When he had lifted the catch the iron door opened easily enough, though with an audible protest from unoiled hinges, and he half expected to find some ribald message waiting for him within; a message of mockery from Hogan, taunting him for having allowed himself to be so completely fooled. But though the message was there sure enough, it was not spelt out in words and there was no foolery about it. It was stark, brutal and sickening.

The feet were what he saw first. They were bare, the toes pointing upward. The light inside the oven was poor; the innermost part of it was almost in darkness; but the gloom was not sufficient to hide from Rowan's eyes the body of the woman; naked, lying on her back just as she had been placed there. She was a blonde, rather small and slimly built; no great weight for a man to carry. That much he could see. And it was more than he would have wished to see.

So Hogan had been telling the truth: he was a murderer. Yet he had to be crazy too. For who but a madman would kill a woman, place the body in a wall oven in a derelict house, and then ring up a complete stranger to tell him about it?

Or was it after all simply an elaborate practical joke? The light was dim; so could this be not a genuine corpse but merely a shop window dummy or something of that description?

There was one way of finding out; yet Rowan hesitated to take it; unwilling to make any physical contact with that motionless object lying in the dimness of the oven. It was so much like a corpse in a compartment in a morgue, waiting to be identified. He was aware of a chill in his spine like a trickle of ice-cold water, and he had an urge to slam shut the door of the oven, go to the police, report what he had found and leave them to deal with it.

But what if the thing he was looking at should after all turn out to be simply a dummy? What kind of a fool would he appear to be? The story would get around and he would become a laughing-stock; a man who had been taken in by an anonymous telephone call and could not tell the difference between a genuine corpse and a counterfeit. Could he leave himself open to that kind of banter? The answer was inescapable: no, he could not.

Having come to this conclusion, he stretched out an arm and touched one of the legs with his hand. The limb felt cold and firm under his fingers, but its essential character was not to be doubted: it was human flesh and bone. This was no lay-figure but a dead woman.

He drew his hand away as if it had been stung. He had a feeling of revulsion, even of nausea. He had written a dozen mystery novels and this was the first time he had seen a genuine murdered person. This was no fiction but, as Hogan had said, the real thing.

And he did not like it.

Chapter Three – One of Those Things

HE thought of going back to the cottage and putting a telephone call through to the police. He was half-way there when he changed his mind and decided to drive on to Wingstead and make his report in person.

The Wingstead police-station was a fairly modern red-brick building, and there was a young constable manning the desk just inside the front entrance. No other person was engaging this man's attention when Rowan walked in, and he was able to state his business without delay.

"I have to report a murder."

The constable gave no indication of being at all surprised by this bald statement, though it was unlikely that murder was a crime he came across very frequently in the course of his duties. He seemed to be of a phlegmatic temperament and calmly proceeded to do things according to the book. And according to the book meant first recording Rowan's name and address before taking the matter further.

Rowan had the impression that his opening speech had been received with a certain amount of disbelief, though this reaction was not expressed in so many words; it was simply a hint in the manner of the man and the intonation of his voice. Perhaps in his position you had to deal too often with jokers and cranks, so that you became naturally reluctant to take anything on trust.

It was the same when he related his story to a sergeant. He had to tell it all from beginning to end: the telephone call from Hogan, the clue of the Lazar House, the search there, the finding of the body . . .

"So you are a crime writer, Mr Rowan."

That fact had emerged in the course of his statement, and it was apparent that this sergeant, a burly, crop-headed man named Gray, had never heard of him. He had probably heard of Agatha Christie, even perhaps of Arthur Conan Doyle, but not of Charles Rowan. It was only to be expected. His was not exactly a household name.

"Yes, I am."

Sergeant Gray nodded. "Ah!" It was a non-committal sound. It might have indicated that in his opinion writers were a breed inclined to fantasy, whose words needed to be taken with a generous helping of salt.

Nevertheless, statements such as Rowan had made had to be taken seriously. They had to be checked and not dismissed out of hand simply because they sounded most improbable. And so, shortly after entering the police-station, Rowan found himself in a car seated next to a plain clothes detective constable and being driven back to the Lazar House.

The detective's name was Ryder. He was a cheerful shock-headed young man wearing a tweed jacket and lovat trousers, and he seemed to be perfectly happy with the task that had been given him.

"Don't often get a murder on my patch. Very infrequent in this neck of the woods. Makes a change."

"So you believe I'm telling the truth?"

"Why wouldn't I? I mean to say, there'd be no point in you making up a yarn like that, would there?"

"I might be a crackpot."

Ryder glanced at him and grinned. "Don't look like a crackpot to me, if I may say so. Of course it doesn't have to be murder. Could be death from natural causes."

"You mean the woman may have stripped off her clothes, climbed into the oven and pegged out?"

"Now you're taking the mickey," Ryder said. "No, sir, I didn't mean that. Somebody must have put her in there. Doesn't prove he killed her."

"Hogan said he did."

"The man on the phone?"

"Yes."

"And you believed him?"

"Not at the time. I thought it was a hoax."

"But you couldn't be sure, so you went to the Lazar House to get to the truth of it?"

"Exactly."

"Must have been a bit of a shock, finding the body."

"It was. To be perfectly honest, it made me feel more than a little sick."

"That's understandable. And now do you believe this Hogan character was on the up and up?"

"I have to believe it, don't I?"

"Yes, sir; I suppose you do."

They came to the lane leading to the Lazar House, and it was just as quiet and traffic-free as before. Rowan was directing Ryder, and he indicated the spot just short of the hump-backed bridge where the detective should stop the car.

"It's in that wood on the left."

Ryder parked the car on the weedy verge, and they both got out. With Rowan in the lead, they made their way to the derelict house and went inside. Ryder made no remark on the ruinous state of the building but followed silently at Rowan's heels. When they came to the kitchen Rowan was appalled to see that he had left the door of the oven open. He ought to have closed it, but he had been in such haste to get away that he had omitted to do so; he had left the body in full view for anybody who might have chanced to go in there to see. Yet was it likely that anyone would?

"There it is." He pointed with his finger, staying well back from the oven and its gruesome contents, unwilling to approach any closer.

Ryder had no such inhibitions; he walked to the oven and peered inside. Rowan noticed that he touched nothing; he simply stood there, stooping slightly in order to get a clearer view. He had had the foresight to bring a torch from the car, and he shone the beam into the cavity, revealing in stark detail aspects of the body that Rowan had seen only dimly in the gloom.

But nothing appeared to shock him. He made a kind of humming sound — "Hm, hm, hm!" — as he carried out his inspection, before finally switching off the torch and turning away.

"Was the oven door closed when you found it?" he asked.

"Yes. I opened it and forgot to close it again before I left."

"No reason why you should have closed it. She wasn't likely to walk away." He gave a nod in the direction of the body. "But your prints will be on the catch. You'll need to have them taken at the station for elimination purposes. Not that there's likely to be any others. Your man will have had the sense to wear gloves."

"I suppose so."

"Well, sir," Ryder said, "this is a job for the big boys. I'll have to report back and set the ball rolling."

He used the car telephone for the purpose. When he had finished the call he spoke again to Rowan.

"I've been instructed to stay here until the murder lot arrive. And that, I'm afraid, applies to you too, sir."

It was to be expected, not simply because Rowan's own car was sitting on the tarmac at Wingstead police-station, but also because he would most certainly be required to answer a lot more questions when the so-called big boys arrived. It was well on into the afternoon and he could see that his planned work schedule had been blown completely off course. He had Hogan to thank for that.

"They'll be buzzing around here before long like wasps round a jampot," Ryder said. He seemed quite cheerful about it. As he had said, it made a change for him. "They'll be asking you all the questions again, and some more, I'd guess. You'll be kept busy for quite a while yet." Ryder gave a grin. "You don't look any too happy about it, sir."

"I'm not. It's a damned nuisance."

"That's the reward for finding a corpse. Your time's not your own afterwards. Better not make a habit of it."

Ryder was quite a joker in his way. Rowan gave him a sour look. "I have no intention of doing so. I didn't intend finding this one. I never expected to. I thought the telephone call was a hoax."

"But you had to make sure?"

"Of course I had to make sure. How could I have left it at that?"

"Don't suppose you could. It's just one of those things. Nine times out of ten it's the unexpected that crops up and gives you a kick in the teeth."

Rowan doubted the truth of that, but he did not argue; there would have been no point in it. He just hoped the murder lot would not be too long in arriving. Until then he had to hang around twiddling his thumbs. Which was not his idea of a well-spent afternoon.

*

They were there rather sooner than he had feared they might be. He was sitting on the parapet of the hump-backed bridge, idly gazing at the water as it flowed sluggishly past below, when he heard the first car arrive. It stopped and two men got out. He left the bridge and walked back to where Ryder was speaking to the newcomers. Ryder introduced him to them.

"This is Mr Rowan, who found the body."

They both looked at him in that assessing, vaguely suspicious manner that policemen had even when they were in plain clothes, as these two were. The older one was a tall man, rather thin, slightly round-shouldered, with prominent cheekbones and hair turning grey; he was wearing a dark suit and well-polished black shoes.

"I'm Detective Chief Inspector Wint," he said. "And this is Detective Sergeant Bilton." He indicated his companion.

Bilton gave a nod. He had an athletic look about him; one could imagine him being good at outdoor games; his face was tanned, as if he had just returned from a holiday in the sun, and he was handsome enough to have made his mark on the stage or in films if acting had been his line of work.

Wint gave a faint sigh. "Better take a look at the body then." He spoke resignedly, as of a task that was not greatly to his taste but which had to be done. "If you'll lead the way, Mr Rowan."

They left Ryder with the cars to wait for the rest of the team, and Rowan conducted the other officers to the kitchen. Once again he stayed at a respectable distance from the oven as Wint and Bilton each took a look at the body; neither of them making any comment. No doubt, Rowan thought, they had seen that kind of thing before and accepted it as a natural part of the day's work.

Wint turned to Rowan. "This is just as you found it?"

"Yes. Except that the oven door was shut. I opened it."

"I believe you were told about it by a man who rang you up. Is that so?"

"Yes."

"And he told you where to look for it?"

"Only vaguely. He said he'd give me a clue. And then he said: 'The Lazar House'."

"Just that? Nothing else?"

"No. He rang off then."

"If he knew about the Lazar House," Bilton put in, "it looks like he could be a local man. Who else would even have heard of the place?"

This had already occurred to Rowan. "It also had to be somebody who knew I was a writer, knew where I lived and the telephone number."

"He could've got the number from the phone book if he had the rest of it. You're in the book, are you sir?"

"Oh, yes."

"There you are then."

"Maybe it's somebody you've met," Wint suggested. "Do you know many people in these parts?"

"Very few as a matter of fact. It's only a couple of years or so since I moved down here. Most of my friends live in London."

"Hardly likely to have been a friend, I'd say."

"I suppose not."

The sound of more vehicles arriving outside could be heard. Before long the kitchen had become quite crowded. The photographer was taking flashlight snaps of the body in the oven. Then the surgeon arrived, a fussy little man with a greying beard and horn-rimmed glasses. His name was Cartwright. It was not until he was there that the corpse was at last taken out of the oven.

Rowan had a clearer view of it now than he had had before. It was evident that the woman had been quite young and might not have been unattractive when alive. But the method of killing had done nothing to improve her looks. She had been strangled, and some kind of ligature had been used for the purpose; it had left its mark on the neck, a brown circle below the chin. The face was swollen and there had been some bleeding from the nose. The blood had dried on the upper lip, giving the appearance of a small moustache. A day or two ago she had been a living breathing person; now she was just an inanimate object, something to be examined and handled by perfect strangers: no dignity left, no privacy, no rights of any kind.

He heard Wint's voice in his ear. "Do you recognise her?"

Rowan shook his head. "No. I've never seen her before today."

He had had enough of it. He felt oppressed by the atmosphere in the kitchen. It was all very well for these others; they were the professionals and they had a job to do. But there was no job for him and he felt the need for fresh air.

He spoke to Wint. "I'm going outside. I'm not needed here, am I?"

Wint seemed to understand. "Getting you down, is it?"

"Frankly, yes."

"All right then. You don't have to stay in here. But don't wander away, will you, sir. We need to do some more talking. It's not finished yet."

"I didn't imagine it was," Rowan said. Things like this were not quickly finished. And he had become involved; Hogan had seen to that. Perhaps it had been his purpose. But why? And who the devil was Hogan, anyway?

There was a uniformed constable out in the lane, keeping an eye on the parked vehicles and no doubt prepared to turn away anyone who might come along and feel curious about what was going on. Rowan had no wish to talk to him, so he strolled down to the hump-backed bridge and again contemplated the sluggish stream below.

Time passed; the afternoon wore on; cars came and went. He wondered why it was taking so long to bring the body out of the Lazar House, but no doubt it was all a question of going through the regular procedure, which could not be hurried. Teams of officers were combing the wood for possible evidence, such as the ligature that had been used to kill the victim. Others would be searching the rooms of the house and the outbuildings, leaving, as the cliché had it, no stone unturned.

At last, after a considerable length of time, something appeared to be happening. He returned to the parked vehicles and found that the corpse was being brought out in a body-bag for transport to the mortuary and further examination by the pathologist.

It was at this moment that Major Parkin arrived on the scene in his Range Rover. Major Edward Millhouse Parkin was a retired army officer who lived in Astley Manor, an old country house not far from the village of Little Madding. Rowan knew him by sight, and had in fact been introduced to him at a social evening at the manor which had been arranged by the local Conservative Association. The MP for the constituency had been there to whip up enthusiasm among the faithful, and if possible the unfaithful as well, and Rowan had reluctantly allowed himself to be persuaded to attend by an ardent member of the association named Hilda Westley.

Mrs Westley, a stout gushing woman with an outlandish taste in clothes, had called on him at Flint Cottage with a copy of his latest book which she begged him to autograph for her. He had felt obliged to invite her in and listen to her flattery, and before she left she had managed to sell him a ticket for the social evening. It was of no avail to protest that he was not a political animal; she brushed this objection aside with a majestic sweep of the hand.

"Oh, but I am sure in your heart you are one of us, Mr Rowan. A man of your intellectual quality could hardly not be."

In the end, despairing of getting rid of her in any other way, he bought the ticket. He had no intention of making use of it, but a desire to see the inside of Astley Manor eventually got the better of his reluctance and he went along. He had not been there two minutes when Mrs Westley pounced on him and insisted on introducing him to their host, Major Parkin, as "Mr Charles Rowan, the well-known author who has come to live amongst us, you know."

It was manifestly evident that Parkin did not know, and indeed had never even heard of Charles Rowan, the well-known author; though he did not say so. He turned his somewhat bulbous eyes on Rowan, uttered a curt

"How d'do?" and offered a pudgy hand which made only the briefest of contacts with that of his guest before being withdrawn.

The major was a small man, who seemed to have an inflated idea of his own importance. Rowan had not cared for him at that first meeting and at this second one discovered no reason to alter his opinion. There was a strutting arrogance about the man which was not endearing.

Apparently Wint had not previously met him, but it took him very little time to make himself known to the chief inspector.

"Parkin. Major. This is my property. Local police tell me there's been a murder. That correct?"

"It is, sir."

"Is that the body?" He pointed towards the long parcel which the men were loading into the vehicle that had come for it.

"Yes, sir. It was in the old building."

"The Lazar House. Yes, they told me. Damn bad show. A woman, eh?"

"That's so."

"Planted there by the murderer, I suppose. Damned nerve."

It was the audacity of the act that seemed to incense him most; as if he felt that it was a desecration of his property. He noticed Rowan and addressed him. "Don't I know you? Aren't you the writer chappie?"

"Yes. We met at your house. A party political gathering."

"Ah, of course. Remember now. So it was you who found the body?"

"Yes."

"What the devil were you doing in the Lazar House?"

"Looking for it."

Parkin stared at him. "Looking for it! What made you think you'd find one there?"

"A man rang me up. Told me he'd killed somebody and suggested I should look inside the Lazar House. At that time I had no idea you owned it."

"This is all part of the manor estate. But why on earth should this man tell you about the killing?"

"I've no idea."

Parkin again stared hard at Rowan, as though finding this hard to believe. "Deuced odd. Don't know what things are coming to these days. People seem to have no respect for property. He was trespassing, you know."

Rowan had difficulty in resisting the urge to burst out laughing. It was grotesque. He said: "I doubt whether a man who'd committed a murder would be too much bothered about a small matter like trespass."

Parkin snorted. "You may call it small. I don't." He turned to Wint. "How long are your people going to be here?"

"A bit longer," Wint said. "We're still searching for anything that might give us a lead. But it's unlikely that we'll find anything. It's my opinion that the victim was dead before she ever got here. Even if she wasn't, the murderer would have taken away the clothes and everything else. He'd be cunning enough for that."

"Even if he was mad?" Rowan asked.

"In my experience," Wint said, "it's often the nutters that are the most cunning of the lot."

*

It was evening before Rowan had been ferried back to the Wingstead police-station where his car was still parked; and even then it was some considerable time before he could get away. An incident room had been set up in the station building and the investigation was being headed by a detective chief superintendent named Dwyer; a middle-aged, bald-headed man, very neatly dressed and looking more like a successful lawyer than a policeman. For his benefit Rowan had to repeat yet again the story of the telephone call and his search of the derelict Lazar House; and he was really getting pretty sick of it.

He wondered whether Dwyer believed him. He was beginning to wonder whether anyone believed him. Even to himself the mysterious character going by the name of Hogan seemed more and more unreal. It occurred to him that he himself might be regarded as a prime suspect, even though it was he who had reported the finding of the body. Maybe in the suspicious minds of the lawmen that in itself might be regarded as a fiendishly cunning way of misleading the investigators.

It was coming up to eight o'clock when he was at last allowed to depart, and he drove back to Flint Cottage in a none too happy frame of mind; because he knew that this was not the end of the matter for him, not by a long chalk. He would be harassed now; not only by the police but also by the press. It was bound to happen; he could see it coming. And how the devil was he to get on with his work in such circumstances? Besides which, he was pretty certain he had not heard the last from Hogan; the man would be in touch again; you could count on that.

When he arrived at the cottage he saw that there was a white Mini standing on the gravel, and he remembered then that Julia had planned to come down for the weekend. With so much else on his mind he had completely forgotten the fact until this moment. It was fortunate that she had her own key to the front door and could let herself in, but he guessed that she would be far from pleased not to find him there to welcome her; especially if she had been waiting for any length of time. Well, that was just too bad. It was not his fault.

And it was not his fault that a blissful weekend for two looked like being little better than a disaster. It was just another one of those things.

Chapter Four – Phantom

SHE was in the kitchen when he went in — cooking. She had opened a bottle of wine and he could see by the level that she had been drinking quite a bit of it. Which was fair enough, because he had kept her waiting and she was not going to do any more driving that day.

"So you're home at last, you bastard," she said before he even had a chance to kiss her. "Do you know what time it is? I've been thinking of ringing the police and reporting you as missing. Where on earth have you been?"

"I've been with the police," Rowan said.

"Is that meant to be a joke?" She sounded unamused. And disbelieving.

"I only wish it was. But it's the honest-to-God truth."

She must have realised how serious he was, and her tone changed at once to one of concern. "Something's happened, hasn't it? Tell me."

"Yes, something has happened. There's been a murder."

She stared at him. "A murder?"

"Yes."

"But I don't understand. What could that possibly have to do with you?"

"I'm involved."

"But that's crazy. How can you be? I don't believe it. I mean, who was murdered?"

"I don't know who she was. A woman; that's all I know about her, that she was a woman."

"You're not telling me you killed her? No, that would be just too wild."

"No, of course I didn't kill her."

"Then how for God's sake are you involved?"

"I found the body."

"You found it? Where?"

"Look," he said, "I'll tell you all about it, but first give me a glass of that wine. I'm tired and thirsty and I haven't eaten a thing since lunch. What's that you're cooking?"

"Never mind what I'm cooking. I want to hear how you've come to be mixed up in the murder of a woman." She poured a glass of wine and handed it to him, "Drink that and tell me all about it."

He drank some of the wine and sat down on one of the kitchen chairs. "It all started with this man ringing me up."

"What man?"

"He said his name was Hogan. Or rather he said that was what I could call him. It's pretty obvious now that it wasn't his real name."

"Why is it obvious?"

"Because no man who tells you what he told me is going to give that sort of information away."

Rowan drank some more of the wine. Julia watched him, frowning slightly.

"What was the information?"

"Well, at first there wasn't any. He began by making out that he was just ringing up to tell me how good he thought my last book was. That sort of thing."

"You mean he was a fan of yours?"

"That's what it sounded like at first. But then he said something pretty odd. He said I could do better — plotwise, that is. And he said he could help me."

"With a plot?"

"Yes."

"You've had that kind of offer before, haven't you? You told me so."

"Yes. But this was very different from the usual sort of offer. He said that what he was talking about was not fiction at all but the real thing. And then he said he was a murderer."

"He actually told you that?"

"He certainly did."

"Did you believe him?"

"No, I didn't. I thought he was a joker. I told him so. But he said he'd convince me he was telling the truth by giving me solid proof — the dead body. Or at least he would give me a clue to where I could find it."

"What was the clue?"

"The Lazar House."

She looked puzzled. "That's supposed to mean something?"

"It's an old ruin that was used for lepers years ago. It's half hidden in a wood not far from here."

"I see. So you went to this Lazar House?"

"I had to. I couldn't leave it at that."

"And that's where you found the woman?"

"Yes. Naked. In a wall oven."

"Oh, my God! How absolutely awful! For you, I mean."

"It wasn't pleasant," Rowan admitted. "I write about such things, but it doesn't help when you come across the genuine article. It's one hell of a shock."

"I can imagine it would be." She put a hand on his arm, sympathetic, concerned; perhaps worried too, he thought. "How had she been killed?"

"Strangled. I didn't realise it at the time, but when the police took the body out for the doctor or pathologist or whatever he was to examine it I could see the mark of the ligature on her neck."

"So this Hogan really is a killer?"

"Seems like it."

"But why would he tell you? Where was the point in doing that?"

"I don't know. It's a puzzle. Maybe I'll learn more when he gets in touch again."

"You think he will?"

"I'm sure of it. Even if he is crazy there must be some kind of plan in his mind. And I'm part of it."

She frowned again. "I'm sorry about this, Julia. It's a tough break for you. I mean it looks like being a pretty foul weekend. If I'd known what was going to happen I'd have rung up and put you off. It would have been better if you'd stayed in London."

"Oh, nonsense," she said. "If you're in trouble this is where I should be, lending support."

He glanced at her sharply, not caring much for the expression she had used. "Why should you think I'm in trouble?"

"Well, perhaps that was not quite the right word. Though it is going to be a bother for you, isn't it?"

"Yes, it is."

"But at least it's not as if you're a suspect or anything nasty like that."

"I wouldn't be so sure. I had a feeling now and then that they hadn't crossed me off the list."

"But that's ridiculous. How could they possibly suspect you? It was you who told them where the body was. If you hadn't they wouldn't have known a thing about it."

"They may figure that those who hide can find."

Her concern seemed to deepen. "You're not really serious, are you, Charles? You *are* just joking?"

"Yes," he said, "of course. Just joking."

But it was not much of a joke. He had heard better ones in his time, even from stand-up comedians.

*

They were just finishing the meal that Julia had prepared when the telephone rang. It came as an unwelcome intrusion, breaking in on a cosy tête-à-tête.

"Who can that be?" Julia said.

Rowan had a shrewd idea of the answer. "If it's not the police or someone in the double-glazing line, I can make a pretty good guess."

She did not need to ask what the guess might be; he could tell from her expression that she knew.

The telephone went on ringing.

"Don't you think you'd better answer it?" she said.

He felt a strange reluctance to do so, but it would have been stupid not to; you could not simply ignore something like that and hope it would go away. He pushed back his chair and stood up.

"I suppose I had."

The telephone was in his study. It was still ringing when he reached it and picked up the receiver.

"You took your time," Hogan said. "I was beginning to think you weren't at home."

"So it's you again," Rowan said.

"Yes, it's me again. Surprised?"

"Not really. I was expecting it. I went to the Lazar House and found the body, you see."

"I thought you would. Couldn't stay away from it, could you? So now you do believe I was telling the truth."

"Yes, I believe it now. And I know what a murdering bastard you really are."

He heard a chuckle in the receiver. Hogan sounded not in the least put out by the name he had been called; merely amused.

"Shocked you, did it? Oh dear me! A man in your line of business ought to be able to take a little thing like that in his stride. I mean to say, it's the kind of thing you dish up for your readers, isn't it? You're always shocking them. Trying to anyway. Of course you'll say that's different; it's fiction, not fact; just harmless entertainment. But maybe there's not so much difference at that. Mind or matter, if you see what I mean. And don't they just love it either way! They may raise their hands in horror at the latest brutal killing, but they wouldn't miss reading about all the gory details for anything. They revel in it. That you can't deny."

Rowan wondered uneasily whether there was not some truth in what Hogan was saying. People did tend to wallow in that kind of thing. So was he not pandering to the worst of tastes with what he wrote? But no; that was ridiculous. Hogan was just trying to push some of his own undoubted guilt on to others. But it would not work; it made him no less of a monster to reflect that the general public did take a kind of perverted pleasure in reading about murders. The point was that they did not commit them, and wretches like Hogan did. This was what set him aside from ordinary decent persons. This was what made him a pariah.

He ignored Hogan's specious argument and asked a direct question: "Who was she?"

There was another chuckle; it had a loathsome quality about it which made Rowan's flesh creep. "She was nobody; nobody at all."

"That's a physical impossibility. Everybody has to be somebody. You know that."

"Well, what did she look like to you?"

"She looked like a victim."

"A loser, you should have said. There are a lot of losers in this life. She was one of them."

"So you're not going to tell me?"

"Let the police figure it out. That's what they're paid for."

"I don't understand you," Rowan said. "Why have you chosen me to confide in? What's your motive, for God's sake?"

"Ah, motive! That's what they always look for, isn't it? But suppose there is no motive? In that case there's no peg to hang their inquiries on, is there? They're working in the dark; feeling their way around and getting nowhere."

"You still haven't told me why you picked on me to confide in."

"But I have. Don't you remember? I said I'd give you a plot for your next book."

"And that's the only reason why you rang me up?"

"Of course. What else?"

Rowan did not believe him. There was some other motive; there had to be. Perhaps the man was some kind of secret exhibitionist, if there was such a thing; someone who believed he could achieve notoriety through the medium of the novelist. Maybe Rowan was his chosen link between him and the public.

"I still don't think it's much of a plot."

"Oh, you shouldn't make a hasty judgement. You've only had the start of it so far; the opening chapter, if you see what I mean."

"And there's to be more?"

"You can be sure of that. I promise."

"When?"

"I'll let you know about that. Don't be impatient."

Rowan heard the click as Hogan rang off. There were more questions he would have liked to ask the man, a lot of them. But it was doubtful whether he would have obtained any useful answers. For the present it was Hogan who was calling the shots, and Rowan felt sure he was far too crafty to give away any information that might lead to his own detection. It was a game he was playing, and a very deadly game at that.

Julia had come into the study while he had been talking to Hogan. She watched him put the receiver down.

"It was him?"

"Yes, it was him."

"What did he want?"

"Nothing in particular. I think in a way he was just crowing. I'd followed his lead, you see. I'd found the body and proved that he had been telling the truth."

"So he knew about that?"

"I'm not sure. He didn't say so. He may simply have rung up to check that I'd done it. The fact is I told him even before he had time to ask. I was the one who asked the questions."

"Like what?"

"Like who was the woman?"

"What did he say to that?"

"He laughed and said she was nobody. And before he finished he told me this was only the first chapter. Now I'm wondering just how many chapters there are going to be in his book."

"You think there'll be others?"

"Yes. He promised me that. And I'd say he could be a man who keeps his promises."

"Isn't there any way of stopping him?"

"There's only one way I can see, and that's to catch the swine. Which could be more easily said than done. Anyway, right now I'd better call the police and tell them he's been in touch again."

He put the call through to Wingstead police-station and he was lucky enough to get Detective Chief Inspector Wint on the line. Wint was obviously working late on the murder case. He listened to what Rowan had to relate and then said he would come out to Flint Cottage at once.

Rowan could see no reason why the chief inspector should wish to call on him in person when everything could have been said over the telephone, but perhaps Wint was one of those people who felt the need to be active, even if the activity was not really essential to progress. Rowan did not particularly want to have the man walking in on him and Julia at that late hour, but he made no objection.

He rang off and told Julia. "He's coming to see me."

"Who is?"

"The chief inspector. Name of Wint."

"Is that necessary?"

"He seems to think so, and I could hardly refuse. If you don't want to meet him you can go to bed."

"Don't be stupid," she said. "Of course I want to see him."

Wint arrived in less than fifteen minutes. They heard his car stop outside, and Rowan had opened the door before he could ring the bell. He took the detective into the sitting-room where Julia was waiting, and he made the introduction.

"Julia Spence. Miss Spence is here for the weekend."

"Ah!" Wint said, giving her a keen glance. "I imagine Mr Rowan has told you all about what's been going on?"

"Yes, Chief Inspector, he has. Not a very pleasant story."

"Murder never is, in my experience, Miss Spence."

"I imagine not. I suppose you don't mind if I sit in on your talk with Charles, do you?"

Wint appeared to hesitate a moment, then shrugged. "I see no reason why you should not."

She offered him a drink, which he refused, and a chair, which he accepted.

"So, Mr Rowan, this fellow Hogan has been in contact with you again. He didn't waste much time. Did he know you'd found the body?"

"I can't be sure. I'm afraid I jumped the gun and told him I had. But how could he have known?"

"We've issued a press statement. Very brief. It was too late for the evening papers but it could have been on the later TV and radio bulletins. You haven't seen or heard anything?"

"No. We haven't had either the television or the radio on. Did you mention my name in the handout?"

"No. We thought we'd keep that under wraps for the moment. Otherwise you'd have had the newshawks knocking on your door or ringing you up. It'll happen of course. We'll have to give a few more details tomorrow and they're bound to be down on you. Take my advice and tell them as little as possible."

"You haven't found out who the woman was, I suppose?"

"Not yet. Could be difficult. No clothes, no belongings of any kind to identify her. We'll issue a photograph and put out an appeal for anyone in this area that knows of a young woman gone missing recently to come forward. And tomorrow we'll start house to house inquiries and hope for the best. Somebody may have seen something, like a car parked near the Lazar House; but it's likely Hogan dumped the body there during the night when few people would be about."

"Do you know how long she'd been dead?"

"Probably less than twenty-four hours, according to the pathologist's estimate. What did Hogan say to you?"

"Nothing of any use to you, I'm afraid. It's odd, but his main purpose seemed to be to mock me."

Wint looked surprised. "To mock you? In what way?"

"Well, for one thing, he said a man in my line of business ought not to be shocked at finding a dead body and so on. And he just laughed when I called him a murdering bastard."

"You called him that?"

"Yes; and it seemed to amuse him. He may even have taken it as a compliment."

"Did you ask him who the woman was?"

"Yes."

"He didn't tell you, of course?"

"No. That would have been too much to expect, wouldn't it? He just said she was nobody."

Wint nodded. "There are a lot of nobodys about. The big cities are full of them; runaways, loners, misfits. If they vanish no one cares; no one even reports them missing. She could have been one of that sort. Seems likely."

"Which makes things difficult for you."

"Exactly."

Julia put in a question. "Do you think he's mad?"

Wint gave it some thought before answering. Then: "It depends on what you mean by mad."

"Well, if he's killing for no purpose; just for kicks, as you might say —"

"He still might not be certifiably insane. And we don't know for certain that he is doing it for kicks. In his own mind he may have a purpose that seems perfectly reasonable to him and which he hasn't revealed."

"And in that case I suppose the purpose could be something connected with Charles."

"That would certainly appear to be conceivable. Frankly, I would find it hard to believe that he picked Mr Rowan completely at random, just because he happens to write crime novels." Wint turned to Rowan. "Did he give any indication that he had carried out any previous murders?"

"No. I may be wrong, of course, but I somehow got the impression that this was the first."

"But he didn't actually say it was?"

"No. It was just a feeling. It was as if — well, this may sound crazy — but it was as if it was all being done for my benefit. In fact, the first time he rang up he said he wanted to help me."

"Killing for your benefit," Wint said. "Now that is an interesting theory. Can't say I've ever come across anything of the sort before."

Rowan could not be sure whether he was being sarcastic or not. The chief inspector's bony face was as expressionless as his tone of voice, giving no clue to what was passing in his mind.

"I suppose it does sound rather far-fetched."

"Mr Rowan," Wint said, "you can take it from me that whatever Hogan's purpose in all this may be, it most certainly is not to do you a kindness. So let's forget about that, shall we?"

Rowan felt well and truly put down. This tough stringy old policeman, without using those precise words, had quietly told him not to be a fool. With his wealth of experience of the ways of villains he knew what he was talking about; and he might have gone even further and advised Rowan to leave the romantic theorising for his works of fiction.

"I suppose," Wint said, "he didn't give any hint of what his next move might be?"

"Nothing solid. What he did say was that this killing was only the first chapter of the book and that there would be more. He promised me that."

"Which means he intends to strike again. But where and when? That's the big question."

"And he didn't give me the answer to that one."

Wint eventually left, having persuaded Rowan to go over the entire account yet once more from start to finish, just in case there had been anything of significance which they might have missed. But nothing new came up.

"Do you still think he suspects you?" Julia asked, after the sound of Wint's car had faded away in the distance.

"No," Rowan said. "I'm pretty sure he now accepts that Hogan really does exist. Maybe he did all along. Maybe I was just imagining they had me in their sights."

"Perhaps men in his profession always give that impression when they're asking questions. I'm sure if I was being interrogated by a hard-nosed policeman I'd begin to feel guilty even if I knew I was perfectly innocent."

"I believe it's not unusual. It's the real hardened villains, guilty as hell, who don't turn a hair. They're used to lying their heads off in that sort of situation."

"I wonder what Hogan is like. Is he a hardened villain? Did you get any picture in your mind from hearing his voice?"

Rowan thought about it and shook his head. "Not really. Someone coarse and brutish perhaps; but that's simply a deduction from knowing what he's done, nothing to do with the voice. One tends to think of a murderer in that way, but few of them in fact come anywhere near the Bill Sykes stereotype."

"He'd need to be very strong to strangle somebody, wouldn't he?"

"Not remarkably so, I'd imagine. Especially if the victim was a woman as in this case. And using a ligature would not be like strangling with the bare hands."

"It gives me the shivers to think of him somewhere out there." She made a gesture in the direction of the curtained window. "Lurking in the darkness like a phantom."

"Oh, come now," Rowan said. "You're letting your imagination run away with you. There's no reason to suppose he's out there. He could be miles away, and probably is."

Nevertheless, he could not help thinking that she had picked the right word. He was a phantom that had come to haunt them.

Hogan the phantom.

Chapter Five – Press Gang

WHEN Rowan came to think about it, he had to admit that he knew surprisingly little about Julia, even though they had been lovers for almost a year. She seemed reluctant to talk about herself, as though it were a subject that was of no great interest to her and she could not imagine why it should be of much concern to anyone else. He wondered sometimes whether this was a pose or whether she was secretive by nature and resented any probing into what she regarded as nobody's business but her own.

Not that Rowan had any desire to probe; he was perfectly happy to accept her as she was: a highly attractive young woman with whom he became ever more enchanted as time went by. Whether their mode of living, in what might have been termed a semidetached manner, had anything to do with this continued enchantment, he did not pause to ask himself.

But the fact was that being apart for frequent periods of several days meant that each coming together was like a fresh start to the romance, looked forward to with lively anticipation and all the more intense by reason of its brevity. There was no time to become bored with each other's company, no time to settle down into a repetitive and possibly dull routine, because there was always that recurrent break that would tear them apart until the next ecstatic reunion.

He still urged her to give up the Highgate property and move into Flint Cottage with him, while she still argued that he should abandon his country life and return to the infinitely more inspiring London scene. But gradually the arguments on both sides had become less and less persuasive, a mere form of words that was no more than a ritual in which neither of them any longer believed. Tacitly they seemed to have come to an agreement to leave the present arrangement as it was, a mixture of living together and living apart which had its undoubted drawbacks but on the whole worked well enough.

"I suppose," Julia once said, "there is one great advantage in maintaining two separate establishments."

"And what might that be?" Rowan asked.

"If we should ever decide to call it a day there'll be no complications."

It shocked him to hear her mention such a possibility. "How can you even think of anything like that? I love you, Julia."

"And I love you, my darling. But one has to take a cool view of such matters. Love doesn't always last. One thinks it will at the time; one wants to think so; but there can be no cast-iron guarantee of permanence. That's a hard fact of life, I'm afraid."

He wondered whether she was speaking from experience; it sounded like it. And he did not care for the sound. Though of course the truth of what she had said could not be denied, depressing though it might be.

She had parents living in Sussex; that much she had divulged. But as far as he could tell she never went to see them, and apparently if they ever came up to London they avoided visiting their artist daughter. He gathered that there was some rift between them; and this seemed to be the case too with any other relations she might have had. Her family meant nothing to her. She was an independent.

His own family ties were none of the strongest, though he had brothers and sisters and cousins here and there, as well as parents and uncles and aunts. It was just that he seldom got round to seeing any of them, and few of them ever took the trouble to visit him. The majority probably had no idea where he was living. He sometimes wondered whether any of them bothered to read his books. He had never heard that they did.

He would probably never have known of the existence of Peter Dacre if it had not been for a chance meeting in a Soho restaurant. They had gone up to the West End to see a new play that had had glowing reviews in all the quality papers and some of the other kind too, and were having a meal in an Italian establishment called Pirandello's when this man came over to their table and spoke to Julia.

"Well now, isn't this a pleasant surprise! Julia, how are you? Do you know, I was only this moment thinking of you and wondering how you were getting on. And, lo and behold, you appear before my very eyes. Astounding, isn't it?"

She looked at him, and it was evident to Rowan that she did not share his pleasure in the encounter. She answered coldly: "I see nothing in it. A coincidence, yes; but coincidences occur pretty regularly, don't they?"

"Ah," he said, "that's my Julia. Down to earth as ever."

Rowan felt a sudden wave of resentment at the expression 'my Julia'. What right did this man have to call her that?

"Yes," she said. "As ever. Did you imagine I would have changed since we last met?"

"No." He gave a smile, perhaps faintly teasing. "And who would have it otherwise? Why change perfection?"

She frowned. "Don't be a fool. Don't you see that I am not alone?"

For the first time he condescended to acknowledge her companion's presence. He turned his gaze on Rowan, still with that annoying smile giving a twist to his lips. "Of course. Introductions would perhaps be in order."

For a moment Rowan thought she was going to refuse, but it would have been childish to have done so. As a compromise she made the introductions as curt as possible.

"Charles Rowan. Peter Dacre."

In his own mind Rowan classified Dacre as a handsome devil and disliked him on sight. He was black-haired and clean-shaven, tall and lean and elegantly dressed. Indeed, there was an overall elegance about him that gave Rowan, much to his own annoyance, a feeling of inferiority. In comparison he felt suddenly gauche and ill-dressed. Dacre looked to be about thirty-five or possibly even a well-preserved forty, and he was wearing what might have been an old school tie. He said:

"I'm very pleased to make your acquaintance, Charles."

He offered his hand, and Rowan felt compelled to take it. There was in Dacre's clasp a suggestion of latent strength which was quite surprising. Rowan looked into his eyes and tried to read something in them, but encountered only a kind of invisible veil, a barrier between him and the man's inmost thoughts.

He released the hand and Dacre let it fall to his side. The tinkle of crockery, the hum of conversation, the aroma of Italian cooking, all mingled to form a background to this unlooked for meeting which at least one of the participants would all too evidently have preferred not to have taken place.

She was making no attempt to keep the conversation going. Indeed, she was giving every indication short of a downright statement of the fact that Dacre was not welcome there, and the sooner he left the better she would like it. The message was plain enough, but he chose to take no notice of it.

Dacre addressed Rowan. "And what is your line of business, may I ask?"

Julia answered for him: "Charles is an author."

"Is that so?" Dacre turned again to Rowan. "What name do you write under?"

Which was just a way of saying that he had never heard of him.

"My own," Rowan said.

"And what sort of books do you write?"

"Crime novels."

"Ah! Well, of course I never read whodunnits." In the way he said this Dacre managed to convey the fact that he looked upon crime writing as an inferior genre, not worthy of an intelligent person's attention.

"Perhaps," Rowan said, "you don't read anything."

Dacre ignored this remark and addressed himself once more to Julia. "Have you two known each other long?"

It was an impertinent question, and she answered with a flash of anger: "That is none of your business."

He grinned, not in the least put out, annoyingly at his ease. The grin revealed the perfection of his teeth; it was as though a cover had been drawn back to reveal those pearly treasures. He turned to Rowan.

"She has a temper. But perhaps you knew that already."

Rowan felt his own temper rising. The man's arrogant rudeness was enough to raise anyone's hackles.

"Don't you think you had better go?" he said.

Dacre remained annoyingly cool. He gave that smile again and a slight shrug of the shoulders. But Rowan thought now that he could detect a hint of venom in the eyes, as though the veil had momentarily been drawn aside; though he still spoke calmly.

"Of course. One must never overstay one's welcome, must one? Au revoir, Julia my sweet. I'll be seeing you again — sometime. Meanwhile, take care, There are so many wolves going around in sheep's clothing these days."

He turned and was gone.

"Damn!" Julia said. "Damn him to hell!"

The rest of the evening was spoiled. Somehow Dacre had put a blight on it. Though neither of them even mentioned his name, he was in their thoughts and they both knew it. Not until they had returned to her house did Julia broach the subject.

"Well?" she said. "Why don't you ask?"

"Ask what?"

"About Peter, damn it. You're aching to know, aren't you?"

"All right," he said. "So tell me."

"We were lovers. He lived with me for a time."

It was no more than he had expected to hear; he had never imagined that he was her first lover, any more than she was his. But somehow, in the few minutes of that brief encounter in the Soho restaurant, Peter Dacre had managed to get completely under his skin, and he could not avoid a feeling almost amounting to disgust that a man like that should have preceded him in her affections.

"How long?" he asked.

"Only a very few months actually."

"What brought it to an end?"

"I threw him out."

It gave him some satisfaction to hear this. It was good to know that it was she who had been the one to break off the relationship.

"Why?"

"Because I came to my senses and realised what a right bastard he really was."

This was better still. Rowan began to feel more cheerful. It was evident that she had no lingering regard for Dacre; no regrets for having finished with him.

"Did he object to being thrown out?"

"As a matter of fact, yes. He objected like hell. Made quite a scene. For one thing, I think it hurt his pride, proved that he was not irresistible. He has a terrible lot of self-esteem, you see."

"Yes, I had that impression. Of course he has some reason. He's got the looks."

She admitted that this was true. "But looks aren't everything. When you live with someone you soon find out what else there is to them. You see behind the mask."

"So he made a fuss when you told him to go?"

"Yes. He refused at first; said I couldn't get rid of him like that. I told him I could get rid of him any way I pleased and I didn't want him around any more."

She did not say what had brought things to a head like this, and Rowan did not ask. Better perhaps not to know.

He said: "I imagine he was still in love with you?" He could understand any man's reluctance to give her up.

"Possibly. But I think he also regarded me as a possession. He had this idea that I belonged to him, just like his car and his wristwatch, and there was no way he was going to let me go. In fact he said as much. That was what made me really angry. I blew my top and told him to go to hell."

Rowan smiled. "I suppose that was what he was referring to when he said you had a temper."

"No doubt."

"The impression I gained was that he still feels possessive where you're concerned and resents anyone else having you. Like me for instance."

"Yes," she said. "I think you're right. I remember the last words he said before he left: 'You're still mine. You'll always be mine. Some day I'll have you back, and God help anyone who stands in my way'."

"He said that?"

"Yes. And he meant it. He really meant it."

"And now I'm standing in his way."

"Yes, you are, aren't you."

He saw that she was frowning. "Does it bother you?"

She admitted that it did. "A little. There's a mean streak in him. No telling what he may do."

"He won't do anything," Rowan said. "It was just an empty threat. The sort of thing people say in the heat of the moment. You'll see. Nothing will come of it."

But he was not so sure of that himself, because he had had that glimpse of venom in Dacre's eyes, and for a woman like Julia what would a man not do?

"What does he do for a living?" he asked.

"Oh," she said, "he doesn't do anything. Well, not much. He's rich, you see. He's on the board of one or two companies, I believe, but it doesn't take up much of his time."

"Nice for him."

*

They were there in force in the morning: the press gang, as Rowan called them. They had got wind now of his involvement in the murder and they wanted all the grisly details. The television people were there too. The road outside Flint Cottage was jammed with vehicles. Seeing them through the window, Julia was aghast.

"My God! They're like a pack of wolves. What do we have to do to get rid of them?"

"We have to give them a story," Rowan said. "At least, I do. You can keep out of the way if you like."

But she refused to do that. "They're bound to find out about me. You know what they're like. Best not to give them the idea that you're hiding something."

He had to agree that she was probably right. Someone was already knocking on the front door. He unlocked it and they went out together to face the mob.

Cameras were clicking, microphones were being waved around, dozens of pairs of feet were trampling the neglected flower beds in the front garden, questions were being fired at him from all directions.

"Who's the lady, Mr Rowan?"

"Miss Spence. She's spending the weekend here."

"Was she with you when you found the body?"

"No. She arrived later."

"This man who called you on the phone. Did he give a name?"

"No."

"You didn't recognise his voice?"

"No."

"What did you feel like when you saw the body?"

"Shocked."

"Whereabouts was the corpse?"

"In a brick oven."

The questions went on. Rowan kept his answers as brief as possible, sticking to the plain facts, refusing to be drawn into any speculations as to who the informant was or the identity of the victim, keeping the name of Hogan a secret, as Wint had instructed him.

"Why did he pick on you to tell, Mr Rowan?"

"I don't know."

"Was it because you're a crime writer?"

"Possibly."

"Will you write a book about it?"

"No."

"Do you think the killer will strike again?"

"I haven't thought about it."

Which was a lie, of course; but why tell them? Let them make their own guesses.

As soon as they could get away from the press gang and the television cameras they went to take a look at the Lazar House. It was Julia's idea; she wanted to see the place where Rowan had found the body. He thought it rather a morbid curiosity but made no objection.

"I doubt whether they'll let you go into the house. But I'll show you where it is."

They decided to go on foot. The weather was fine and it was no great distance. When they reached the lane it became apparent that there were others besides themselves who had felt the urge to visit the scene. There were cars coming and going; more traffic indeed than that narrow roadway had ever accommodated. Not that anyone was being allowed to see much; the way into the wood had been sealed off by the police and there were officers repeating the search of the previous day, no doubt to make certain that nothing had been overlooked.

As he had expected, no one else was being allowed to go nearer than the verge, and the driver of any car that stopped was quickly ordered to be on his way. He and Julia had no sooner reached the spot where he had parked his car during his first visit than an officious uniformed constable brusquely demanded to know their business.

The man was a stranger, so Rowan introduced himself. "I'm the one who found the body."

The constable became at once more affable. Nevertheless, he would not allow them to go any nearer the Lazar House. "Sorry, Mr Rowan, but those are my orders. No one's permitted to leave the road. We've been pretty well overrun with sightseers coming to gawp. Downright ghoulish, I call it. And after all, what is there to see?"

"Have they found any clues?" Rowan asked.

"I don't know, sir. I doubt whether they would tell me even if they had."

"No, perhaps not."

As they were walking away Julia said: "I feel rebuked."

"In what way?"

"I have been accused of being ghoulish. Do I look like a ghoul would you say?"

"I've never seen one," Rowan said. "But I can think of nothing less like the popular conception of a ghoul than you."

She laughed. "Thank you, Charles. You've restored my self-respect."

When they reached the cottage they discovered that the ladies and gentlemen of the television and press had all departed, leaving only the trampled garden as evidence of their visit. There was just one car parked by the front gate with a man sitting in it and smoking a cigarette. This individual turned out to be a technician who had come to connect a recording machine to the telephone, so that any future message from Hogan could be recorded on tape and studied by an expert. Rowan thought it was a bit late; they should have done the job before Hogan's second call had come through. It was a case of shutting the stable door after the horse had bolted. Though of course this particular horse might well come back.

The man did his work and showed Rowan how to switch the recorder on, since it would have been pointless to tape every call that came in. Hogan was the one they wanted.

When the technician had gone Rowan sat down at his desk and had a look at the novel he was working on; but he knew it was going to be no use trying to write any more of it at the present time; there was far too much superfluous traffic jamming the arterial highways of his brain. If Hogan really had been sincere in his expressed desire to help him, he could hardly have chosen a more certain way of achieving the precisely opposite effect.

Julia came in while he was sitting there. "What are you doing?" she asked.

"Nothing."

"I thought perhaps you were working on the new book."

"How can I? I can't even begin to think about it."

She glanced with an expression of disapproval at the chaos on his desk. "You know, Charles, you're terribly unco-ordinated. You ought to use a word processor. I thought all professional writers did these days."

"Not this professional writer. I tried one once but got rid of it. It was no use to me. I can't even use a typewriter for the first draft; the mechanism appears to create a stoppage in my thinking processes. On the other hand, a pen seems to act as a conduit between brain and paper. My thoughts flow through it. Maybe I'm old-fashioned, but that's the way it is. Sometimes, of course, the conduit gets choked up and everything comes to a stop. That's what's called writer's block, which could be another term for sheer laziness. A writer, you know, will do almost anything rather than write. Any excuse will do. Odd, isn't it?"

"Very odd. But since you're so opposed to all things modern I wonder you don't use a quill pen and an inkpot."

"Don't turn your nose up at quills. Many of the world's finest books were written with them. All this modern technology may have made the purely mechanical side of writing easier, but it's done nothing at all for the quality of the finished product. The word processor can't think for you."

"All the same," she said, "I do feel that you ought to be more methodical. You work in a terribly disorganised way."

She was right about that, he thought. The desk, which was in fact an old dining-table, was littered with scraps of paper on which were jotted down ideas for incidents, snatches of dialogue, names for characters, bits of narrative . . . Now and then he would sift through this mass of paper, making use of some of it, consigning some to the wastepaper basket, preserving the rest for future reference. He wrote in ruled notebooks with hard covers and typed the completed manuscript on an Olivetti, revising as he went along. It might not have been the best method in the world; some authors might have regarded it as horribly inefficient; but it was the way he did things. It was indeed the only way he could do things. Floppy disks were not for him.

He supposed the whole room reflected this lack of order. It was crammed with books, many of them copies of his own works in various editions and a dozen different languages; some on shelves, others standing in piles on the floor. There were reference books and dictionaries, old manuscripts, boxes of typing paper, stationery of all kinds, staplers, files, ledgers, jars of pens, bottles of gum, paper-clips, newspaper cuttings, magazines which had been kept for some reason long forgotten, dust everywhere . . .

"It really is a dump in here," she said. "How you can work in such a pickle I really do not know."

"Well, as to that," Rowan told her, "I'd say that you're hardly the one to criticise. I've seen your studio, remember."

She accepted the riposte with a smile. "Okay then. Call it quits. What shall we have for lunch?"

Chapter Six – Notorious

THEY watched the television news at one o'clock and saw themselves being interviewed.

"Oh, my God!" she said. "Now we're famous."

"Notorious might be nearer the mark," Rowan suggested.

"Either way, I don't much care for it. Damn you, Charles. Why did you have to get yourself mixed up in a murder case?"

"I didn't ask to be. I was dragged into it."

"You didn't have to go and find the body."

Which no doubt strictly speaking was true; but could anyone in his situation not have gone? He had had the choice of going or not going, but in reality there had been no choice. Hogan had known that.

Detective Chief Superintendent Dwyer appeared on the screen to appeal for anyone who might have information that could be useful in helping to solve the case to come forward or get in touch by telephone. The number to ring was shown and read out.

"Do you think anyone will come forward?" Julia asked.

"Oh, I expect so. They usually get plenty of people to accept an invitation like that. Some are just exhibitionists trying to grab a slice of the limelight. Most of the information is useless, but occasionally something helpful emerges. It's worth a try."

*

Later in the afternoon they locked the cottage and drove into Wingstead in Rowan's car. It was a Saturday and there were plenty of people on the streets, all of them probably well aware that the body of a murdered woman had been discovered not far out of the town. It would be the subject of conversation in pubs and other places where citizens gathered together. And they would discuss it with gusto and not without a certain amount of enjoyment; an event like this brought a sense of excitement into their lives and a perverse feeling of pride in being almost, as it were, involved in a case of unlawful killing which had some bizarre and even salacious features about it. It put Wingstead on the map.

Rowan wondered whether he and Julia would be recognised as they went about their shopping, but no one seemed to connect them with the couple who had appeared on the television screen. Perhaps none of these people had caught the one o'clock news. Only the woman at the check-out desk in the supermarket gave them as much as a second glance. She seemed startled for a moment and about to say something, but thought better of it and got on with her job.

"Perhaps we don't look remarkable enough to stick in people's minds," Rowan said. "Just a couple of very ordinary persons going about their humdrum business."

"So you think I am very ordinary?"

"Well, no. Far from it in fact. But you don't look like someone who would have anything to do with a pretty sordid murder."

"I didn't have anything to do with it."

"No, of course you didn't. But you know what I mean."

"Sometimes," she said, "I'm not at all sure that I do."

*

They paid a visit to the police-station and found Detective Sergeant Bilton there. He told them that the police were making house-to-house inquiries; the kind of routine work that went with a murder investigation.

"Any result?" Rowan asked.

"Not yet. We're still trying to discover whether any young woman has gone missing in the last week or so — or even longer. We've been taking in the villages in the area too, but so far nothing's come of it."

"Anything from the pathologist?"

"Only that no evidence of rape has been found. And apart from some slight bruising no injury at all except to the neck."

"So you still haven't identified the victim?"

Bilton shook his head. "She's a mystery woman. And of course if you can't discover who it is that's been killed it makes it all the harder to find the killer. It begins to look like we'll have to wait for him to contact you again, Mr Rowan."

"And by then he may have struck again."

"That is the danger," Bilton admitted.

*

The early edition of the local evening paper was on sale before they left Wingstead. Rowan bought a copy and they studied it in the car. The murder was front page news and there was a picture of him and Julia with

Flint Cottage in the background. The caption read: 'Crime novelist Charles Rowan with girlfriend artist Julia Spence.'

Julia made a sound that was almost a snort and registered her disgust. "Girlfriend indeed! How I detest that term. When does one became mature enough to be spared such a ridiculous description?"

"Never," Rowan said. "The newspaper scribblers describe women of fifty or even older as girlfriends. Boyfriends can be pretty aged too. It's the custom, I'm afraid."

He scanned the report quickly. There was nothing new in it; nothing they did not already know. The reporter mentioned the titles of a few of his books. One of them was spelt incorrectly. It was about par for the course.

*

That evening the telephone rang. When he answered it a man's voice said:

"I've got another body for you, Mr Rowan."

It did not sound like Hogan, though it could have been him trying another disguised accent, just for the hell of it.

"Who are you?" Rowan asked.

"You know who I am," the man said.

"No, I don't know. Tell me."

"I'm your friend. The one that tells you where to find the corpses. I've given you one; now there's another. Do you want me to tell you where it is?"

"I'd rather you told me your name."

"But you know my name. I told you before, didn't I?"

"Maybe you did; but I've forgotten it. Tell me again. Jog my memory. Make my day."

"All right," the man said. "I'm Satan."

"Get off the line and stop wasting my time," Rowan said. "Go back to whatever wormhole it was you crawled out of, Satan, and don't bother me again."

He rang off, fuming.

"Who was it?" Julia asked.

"Some joker trying to hoax me into going on a fool's errand hunting for another body."

"Not Hogan?"

"No, not Hogan. Didn't even sound like him. And of course he didn't know the name."

51

Wint had told him to be prepared for this sort of thing. There were always cranks around who got some kind of kick out of muscling in on a murder investigation. Sometimes they would walk into a police-station and confess to having committed the crime. Usually it was easy to eliminate them because they were not aware of certain facts that only the true murderer would know; facts purposely not revealed to the news media by the investigators. In this particular case nobody had been told that Rowan's informant was using the name of Hogan. Rowan himself had been warned not to mention it to the press and he had passed the warning on to Julia.

"Will there be more of them, do you think?"

"I shouldn't be surprised."

In fact there was only one other, and Rowan dealt with him as curtly as he had with the first. The genuine Hogan remained silent; he had obviously said all he intended saying for the present and had withdrawn into the shadows, a sinister formless presence that could only be imagined from the sound of a disembodied voice on the telephone.

"When will he contact you again, do you think?" Julia asked.

"Not until he has something interesting to tell me."

"You mean another murder?"

"Yes. He's not likely to ring me up for a cosy little chat. He'll be lying low now. The question is, for how long?"

"It's horrible to think about. Do you realise that somewhere out there is another woman — it's bound to be a woman, isn't it? — another woman, alive and well going about her own affairs, probably with no knowledge whatever of Hogan, who's going to be murdered by him and left somewhere for you to find?"

"Yes, I do realise it."

"And there's nothing we can do to stop it happening."

"Nothing at all. Because we haven't the faintest idea of who he is."

"It makes the blood run cold." She shivered, as if from a sudden chill. "That woman could be me, you know."

"Now stop it, Julia," Rowan said. "There's no need to imagine anything like that. Why would he touch you? He doesn't even know you exist."

"But of course he does. Do you think he hasn't read the papers or watched the TV news? Oh, he'll know about me all right. You can bet on that."

"Well, even if he does, there's no reason to suppose he'll want to kill you. Why should he?"

"Why should he want to kill anybody? He's a nutter; you said so yourself. He doesn't have to have a reason."

Rowan could hardly deny the truth of this. And now that he came to think about it he wondered uneasily whether Julia might not have some cause for alarm, or at least a certain disquiet. She was close to him, and he for some reason or other was the one chosen by Hogan to be his confidant. So might not his odd twisted brain turn its attention to her and view her in the light of a possible future victim? Who could tell? Who could peer inside that brain and read what messages it was sending to the body? Who even knew who Hogan was? Nobody.

"Anyway," he said, "he doesn't know where you live, so you'll be all right there. And you've got locks; don't forget to use them. You're safe enough here with me, and really I'm sure he's not at all likely to even think of you as a possible victim. You aren't really worried about it, are you?"

"No. It was just a thought. But you're right; it's most unlikely. After all, he's your pal, isn't he? He wouldn't want to do anything to harm you — like knocking off the girlfriend."

She was making a joke of it, but Rowan could tell that the uneasiness was there nevertheless. That shadowy menace called Hogan, lurking somewhere in the background, had taken a grip on her imagination and could not simply be laughed away.

"Perhaps I should ask Wint to do something about protecting you. What do you say?"

She shook her head. "It would be a waste of time, wouldn't it? For one thing, I doubt whether he'd be convinced I'm at risk. I'm not convinced of it myself. And even if he was, what could he do? Ask the Metropolitan Police to put a guard on my house? Fat chance. I wouldn't want it anyway. No, Charles, forget it. I'll be all right."

He hoped so. But she had him worried now. Until she had made the suggestion it had never occurred to him that there might be any risk to her from Hogan's madness; now he could not get the thought out of his head. And all this because of that man. Damn him! Damn him, whoever he was!

*

Ursula Wheatcroft rang up later that evening — from her home, not the office. Ursula was a literary agent who handled his work. She was senior partner in the firm of Wheatcroft and Stammers, which was one of the newer agencies, with an address in Essex Street just off the Strand. Ursula was little more than thirty and Jean Stammers was even younger; they had energy and enthusiasm, and he got on well with them. They gave a more personal service than you might get from one of the bigger and older firms, and he liked that.

Their offices were in an old brick building up two flights of creaking stairs, one on each side of the landing. Daylight made its way in there with some reluctance, and there were piles of manuscripts all around, some of which had begun to look rather dog-eared after going on their travels to various publishers and coming back with the usual expressions of regret. Seeing these manuscripts always made Rowan think sympathetically of the authors who had expended so much time and labour on them, and had such high hopes which might in the end be blighted. It was an unforgiving profession, and he sometimes wondered why so many people tried their hand at it and came back time after time in spite of a complete lack of success. Perhaps it was, as Dr Johnson said of a man's marrying for a second time, the triumph of hope over experience.

Ursula said: "I see you've been getting yourself into the news."

"It wasn't my doing," Rowan protested. "I was forced into it."

"By the murderer who told you where to find the body?"

"Yes."

"A very strange affair by the sound of it. Have you any idea what his motive was?"

"I don't think he had one."

"You mean he just picked you out of the blue?"

"Seems like it. Said he'd read my books though."

"Ah, a fan! Well, they come in all shapes and sizes. Anyway, I think we could make use of this."

"You're thinking about the publicity angle, I suppose."

"Of course. It's a windfall."

"No," Rowan said. "Forget it. It's not the sort of publicity I want. I'm involved and I can't avoid that, but I have no intention of trying to profit by it."

"Why on earth not? Surely you're not going to argue that it would be immoral?"

"Maybe I am."

In a way it seemed wrong to turn the murder of a young woman to his own advantage. It was distasteful and he wanted none of it.

But Ursula evidently did not see it in the same light. "What nonsense. I didn't think you were so squeamish, Charles. Anyway, we'll have a talk about it. When are you coming up to town?"

"Next Friday."

"Have lunch with me. We'll sort something out. Okay?"

He had to agree. He was going to spend the next weekend at Julia's place and he could take in the luncheon appointment with Ursula Wheatcroft before going on there.

"Very well, then."

"And please, Charles, don't make it sound so much like a penance. I'll be seeing you."

She rang off and he went back to the sitting-room where Julia was waiting.

"Who was that? Not Hogan this time?"

"No; it was Ursula."

"Oh, the go-getting agent. What did she want?"

"She'd read about the murder."

"And wanted to congratulate you, I suppose."

Rowan was always aware of a certain edginess in Julia when the name of Ursula Wheatcroft came up. Sometimes he wished he had never told her that he had once had an affair with Ursula, though she would probably have found out eventually; somebody would have been sure to tell her, and perhaps it had been better coming from him. It had been soon after Wheatcroft and Stammers had taken him on, some four or five years ago, and it had been quite ecstatic for a time. It cooled later, but there had been no acrimony when it ended; they remained good friends, and as Ursula said, perhaps it was as well that her business relations with him should not get mixed up with the love interest. Affairs of business were best kept entirely separate from those of the heart. He agreed with a certain reluctance, for there had been a while there when he had toyed with the idea of asking her to marry him, and perhaps she would have welcomed the suggestion. Maybe it would have worked and maybe it would have been a disaster; he would never know now.

"She wants me to have lunch with her next Friday."

"Why?"

"To talk business."

"Couldn't you have done that on the phone?"

"It's better face to face."

"And of course it's such a nice face, isn't it?"

"Look, Julia," he said, "we've been over all this before. She doesn't mean anything to me now. Not in that way. She's my agent, nothing else. And a damned good agent."

"Of course. Take no notice of me. I was only teasing."

But he knew that there was more to it than that. Any mention of Ursula was enough to rouse this slight bristling reaction, this hint of jealousy not far below the surface. Perhaps it was the fact that he still had occasional meetings with Miss Wheatcroft that made it difficult for Julia to accept that she was no longer in any sense a rival; perhaps she would have been happier if he had engaged a different agent. But he had no intention of doing that; he doubted whether he could have found a better one and he was not going to try.

The two young women had met. The three of them had had lunch together on one occasion. It had been his idea and a bad one. His hope had been that Ursula and Julia might become friends, but there had never been the slightest chance of that. They had both been icily polite, but it could hardly have been worse if they had used the table knives to stab each other. The friction between them had been so apparent that he could not blind himself to it. He had never repeated the experiment.

"What's the business she wants to discuss?" Julia asked. "Or didn't she say?"

"I think she's got some scheme to make use of the publicity generated by this murder affair."

"To boost your sales?"

"That would be the idea."

"And you're not keen on it?"

"How did you guess that?"

"Oh, my darling, surely you must know by now that I can read your mind. What have you got against it?"

"Only a feeling that it's not quite right somehow. What do you think?"

"I agree with you."

He wondered whether this was an entirely impartial opinion, or whether it had a lot to do with her feeling of antagonism towards the other woman. But he did not put the question.

He said: "I love you, Julia."

"I love you too," she said. "Come hell or high water."

Chapter Seven – Information

SUNDAY was an uneventful day. Even the press had stopped pestering them. Wint paid a call but had little to report. The body was still in the mortuary and it would remain there for the present in the faint hope that someone would turn up to identify it, though Wint thought there was little likelihood of this.

"Maybe we'll never know who she is."

"Hogan could tell you," Rowan said.

"But we don't know who Hogan is, do we?"

"That's true."

"And perhaps we'll never know that either. There's an old saying: 'Murder will out'. It isn't true, you know. Lots of murderers never get caught. They just die of old age."

Detective Chief Inspector Wint seemed to be in a depressed mood. He was not the most cheerful of persons at the best of times, and this was not one of the best. There was a lugubrious look about him, and in his case appearances were not deceptive.

"I suppose he hasn't been in touch with you again?"

"No," Rowan said, "there's been nothing from him. Two jokers rang up yesterday claiming to be him, but they didn't know the name, so I choked them off."

"Ah, that's what you get. It beats me why some people seem to think murder's a joke. It isn't, you know." He stared hard at Rowan, as though accusing him of being one of those people.

Rowan repudiated the implied accusation. "I never thought it was."

"But you write about it."

"Not to make a joke of it."

"But to titillate people, to keep them amused, as you might say. Do you reckon that's legitimate?"

It was not an adjective Rowan had ever thought of applying to his work; it seemed an odd word to use. But he understood perfectly well what the chief inspector meant. He was questioning the ethics of the entire genre of fictional crime writing, the use of what was in fact a pretty sordid and ugly business as the basis of a product aimed at giving the reader a few hours of harmless diversion. But perhaps to a man like Wint it could never be that; perhaps he had had too much experience of the subject at close quarters. He saw the real blood, the gaping wounds, the severed limbs, the battered heads, the unspeakable injuries that could be inflicted by knives and bludgeons and shotguns and axes. How could he be expected to regard any of this as an acceptable source of light entertainment?

"It isn't funny," Wint said. "It's not funny at all."

Rowan thought of arguing in his own defence, but at the moment he could think of nothing convincing to say. This greying officer of the law had the advantage of him and he had to accept it. He thought of mentioning to Wint the misgivings that Julia had regarding her own safety, and decided not to. But he did mention the fact that she would be leaving in the morning. "She has a house in Highgate with a studio where she does her painting."

Wint nodded. "And you will be staying here?"

"Until next Friday. Then I shall join her for the weekend before returning here."

"I see. Perhaps you wouldn't mind giving me that London address, sir. Just so we'll know where to get in touch with you if the need should arise."

"Of course."

"Highgate. That's where Karl Marx was buried, isn't it? In Highgate Cemetery."

"So I believe."

Rowan could think of no connection between Karl Marx's grave and the case in hand, but perhaps Wint had not intended to imply that there was one. Perhaps he was just a Marxist at heart. A Marxist copper! Now there was a thought!

*

They went to bed early and made love. Julia had a body to send a man wild with desire; it certainly had that effect on Rowan. The only fly in the ointment was that sometimes the thought of Peter Dacre came into his head, always bringing with it a stab of jealousy in the reflection that Dacre had been there before him. So maybe he was as bad in that way as Julia, hating the earlier lover; for her part Ursula and for his part Peter. Perhaps it was only human to do so. Perhaps you had to be very civilised not to.

*

She left in the morning, driving the white Mini. He was sorry to see her go; the place seemed to lose some of its brightness without her. He tried to get some work done on the novel, but it was hopeless; he could not get hold of the thread of the narrative; he had difficulty in stringing half a dozen words together. He threw down his pen and went to the kitchen to make a cup of coffee. The progress of his writing could be measured by the number of cups he drank; when it was going badly he became a coffee addict. If he had been a smoker he would probably have taken out his frustration in cigarettes, but he had given up that kind of madness years ago; there were cheaper ways of killing yourself.

The post always came late in that outlying part of the delivery area, and when it came there was nothing but junk mail and a jolly question from the postman who had been unable to push all of it through the letter slot and had had to use the knocker.

"Found any more dead bodies, Mr Rowan?"

Rowan regretted having allowed the man to become so familiar. It had all started with the postman saying he had read some of Rowan's books; and then he had revealed that he was a budding author himself and belonged to Wingstead Writers' Circle, which held monthly meetings in the Guildhall. The postman's name was Josh Froggatt, but he used the penname of Austin Carruthers because he thought it sounded more distinguished. He had never had anything published, but he wrote poetry and short stories and was confident that one day he would make the breakthrough. Now and then he would bring samples of his work for Rowan to read and comment on. Rowan found this particularly distressing because he did not wish to hurt Froggatt's feelings by stating his honest opinion; so he made the mistake of giving the man some guarded praise, which of course only encouraged him to bring more of his literary output.

"No, I haven't found any more," Rowan said.

"Rum old business that," Froggatt remarked. He was a chubby-cheeked young man with a wispy ginger moustache. "You going to use it for one of your novels?"

"I don't think so."

"No? I'd've thought you could've made something of it. Right on your own doorstep and all, as the saying is."

"Perhaps it's a bit too near my own doorstep."

"Ah, I see what you mean. Well, better be on my way."

Froggatt got into his van and drove off, while Rowan shut the door and went to throw the junk mail into the wastepaper-basket, thus rejecting the chance of winning a quarter of a million pounds and a new car and various other valuable prizes that were on offer.

He had another stab at the novel, and nothing came of it. He made some more coffee and ate a biscuit and decided to take a walk to the Lazar House to see what was going on down there. Nothing was. The police had gone; the sightseers had gone. Except for the trampled verge it was just as it had been when he had made his discovery.

Standing there, he tried to imagine the murderer carrying his limp burden into that sombre wood. The police were satisfied that the killing had not been done in the Lazar House or the wood surrounding it. There had been no evidence of a struggle and it was almost certain that the woman had been dead before arriving at that place. In his mind Rowan had the picture of a rough burly man, strong enough to carry his burden with ease.

But who was he — this mysterious Hogan? Someone evidently who had knowledge of the area; a local man perhaps. Someone also who had read some of his books and knew his address. Who fitted this description? A name floated to the surface — Josh Froggatt. Who would be more familiar with the lie of the land than a postman who delivered mail to every house in the district? And Froggatt had read the books and looked strong and maybe was as crazy as a coot.

Rowan stopped himself there. It was ridiculous; impossible to imagine Froggat as a murderer; nobody could have looked less like one. But what did a murderer look like? Was there any standard pattern? Of course not. So could Froggatt possibly be Hogan? Unlikely certainly; but impossible? Perhaps not.

Hogan had said at the outset that he wanted to help Rowan, but had he been telling the truth? Suppose his real purpose had been quite different; suppose he wished rather to harass him. Which was in fact just what he had succeeded in doing; disrupting his work and making it impossible for him to get on with his latest novel. Now who would wish to do something like that? Another writer perhaps? A failed author, envious of his success? Again unlikely, but again not utterly impossible. It would be really crazy to go to such lengths for such a purpose, of course. The killing of a woman just to harass another man; that would indeed be a wild idea. But had he not already concluded that the man was crazy? And madness took many forms.

Froggatt was another writer, Froggatt was not successful with his literary efforts, Froggatt looked strong. Again he stopped himself. He must not let the man become an obsession; that would be as crazy as anything else. So forget Froggatt, and forget his alter ego, Austin Carruthers, too.

*

On the Wednesday he had a visit from Detective Constable Ryder, whom he had not seen since the day when he had discovered the body. Ryder had some news which he thought Rowan would be interested to hear. Though it might come to nothing, the investigators had been given a lead of sorts. A man had walked into the police-station at Wingstead with a piece of information that could have some bearing on the murder case.

The man's name was Zacharia Smith, but he was commonly known as Zak. He was quite a well-known character around the neighbourhood of Little Madding, being a mole-catcher by trade and a one-time poacher. He was in his seventies, never shaved or had his hair cut, wore the oldest of clothes, rode a clapped-out bicycle with a box on wheels as a trailer to carry his tools, looked upon the bath as an invention of the devil and took with him a rich aroma that could be detected at a distance of several yards downwind. He lived by himself in a crumbling thatched cottage, which lacked the blessings of mains electricity and piped water and was situated further down the lane that ran past the Lazar House. And with this primitive existence he appeared to be perfectly contented.

"What," Rowan asked, "was the information?"

"He saw a Range Rover standing by the side of the lane near the Lazar House one night as he was going home. It didn't have any lights on and there was no one in it as far as he could see."

"And why didn't he come forward before?"

"Well," Ryder said, "you may find this hard to believe, but he didn't know we were looking for people to do just that until someone happened to mention it to him in a pub. You see he doesn't have television and he never reads the papers."

"In this day and age. Amazing."

"Isn't it?"

"When was it he saw the Range Rover?"

"It seems to have been a week or so before you found the body, so it couldn't have been when the murderer was putting it in the oven. But of course it could have been him making a survey of the place in advance. He wouldn't have wanted to bring the body and then hunt around for somewhere to hide it. That's the theory, anyway."

"Did Smith see any light in the house?"

"He says he did see a glimmer but didn't take much notice of it at the time, and he certainly wasn't going to investigate. He just wanted to get home and go to bed. My guess is he'd been on the beer."

"So this doesn't get us much further, I suppose."

"Not immediately. But we've been following it up. We've been looking up all the known owners of Range Rovers round about."

"Including Major Parkin?"

Ryder grinned. "Yes. I'm rather glad I didn't have that job."

"I imagine he didn't take kindly to being questioned."

It appeared that the major had been seriously affronted. He had completely lost his temper, demanding to know whether he was being accused of murdering some unknown woman and dumping her body on his own property. Did they really imagine he would be so stupid? Assurances that he was being accused of nothing and that the police were simply carrying out routine inquiries had done little to mollify him.

"He's a very peppery old boy," Ryder said.

Rowan already knew that. "I suppose," he said, "the postman who brings my mail doesn't own a Range Rover?"

The question appeared to surprise Ryder. "Who is your postman?"

"The name is Josh Froggatt. Do you know him?"

"As a matter of fact I do. Why do you mention him? You don't think he's our man, do you?"

"No, of course not. Don't really know what made me ask. Except that he's one of the few persons I know around here."

"Well," Ryder said, "it's a funny thing, that. Froggatt rides a motor-bike; goes to work on it. He's not married and he lives with his brother and the brother's wife on a small farm not far from here. I've just come from there as it happens, because Les Froggatt runs an old Range Rover. I believe Josh uses it sometimes." He gave Rowan a shrewd look. "You're sure there wasn't any particular reason why you asked about him?"

"Oh, quite sure. I mean to say, would anyone in his right mind suspect him of being a murderer?"

"No," Ryder said, "they wouldn't." He paused for a moment, then added: "And they could be wrong."

Chapter Eight – A Big Hand for Charlie

HE picked Ursula up at the office in Essex Street and they had lunch at a vegetarian restaurant above a health food shop in the Strand. Ursula had given up eating meat some time ago after seeing a feature on BBC 2 which showed the way animals were slaughtered and prepared for human consumption. She said she had found it quite revolting, and when you came to think about it there was the moral aspect too: was it right that we should rear these fellow creatures of the planet earth for the sole purpose of butchering them to fill our own bellies?

"So lions and tigers and all the other carnivores are immoral?" Rowan asked.

"They are dumb beasts who know no better," she said. "We do not have to base our conduct on them. We are supposed to have progressed beyond the primitive state. Though sometimes I do wonder."

Rowan had no objection to a vegetarian meal now and then; some of the concoctions he found very tasty. On this occasion they both had a wholemeal pizza with a tomato salad for the main course and something called apricot bourdaloue tart for dessert.

"This is delicious," he said. "And you, if I may say so, are looking very beautiful."

She was petite and dark-haired, and as always smartly dressed. Julia tended to be casual in her dress, but Ursula took great care in her choice of clothes and wore them to perfection.

"Don't I always?" she said.

"Well, as to that, I can't remember any time when you did not."

"And your memory is good?"

"It's excellent. I even remember that once I thought of asking you to marry me."

"I know."

"How could you? I never said anything."

"There was no need. In those days I could read your mind like a cheap novel. Maybe I still can."

63

He remembered that Julia had said much the same thing. So were they both unnaturally intuitive or could anyone do the trick with him?

"Ah!" he said. "And if I had asked, what would the answer have been?"

"It might have been yes. Quite possibly it would."

"And if it had been, would it have worked, do you think?"

"I doubt it. It's better this way. We might have divorced by now, and then you might have gone to another agent. How are things between you and Julia?"

"Fine. Couldn't be better."

"I'm so glad," she said, But he had the feeling that she was not terribly overjoyed at that. Perhaps she would have liked to hear that his love life with another woman was rather less than perfect. And perhaps he was wronging her in thinking so.

It was not until the end of the meal that she broached the subject she had really wanted to discuss with him.

"I've had a talk with Simon Cathcart, and he'll be happy to have you on his chat show."

"But I won't be happy to be on it," Rowan said.

"Now don't be obstinate, Charles. What have you got against appearing on the show?"

"I gave you my reasons on the phone. And besides, I don't like Simon Cathcart. I think he's a toad."

"I didn't know you'd met him."

"I haven't, but I've seen his show, and in my opinion it stinks. It's the absolute nadir of all chat shows. And that takes some doing, I can tell you."

"It has a very big audience. Appearing on it could be very good for sales."

"And that would mean more commission for you, of course."

She flared up at once. He had never seen her look so angry. If they had not been in a public place he felt sure she would have thrown a plate at him. And she might have shouted instead of keeping her voice strictly under control.

"Is that what you think? That all I do for you is with an eye to my own interests. I am your agent, damn it; and in that capacity I have an obligation to get the best deals I can for you. At least, that's the way I see it. But of course if you really believe there's nothing but a selfish motive in what I do, okay. Maybe you'd like to find someone else to nurse you along;

someone else to see you through the bad periods when you can't get going; to tell you what a good writer you are when you have the blues and know you'll never write another stinking word; someone else to be your guide, philosopher and friend. That's if you can find anyone to do the job for peanuts. You're not a gold-mine, you know. You're not Jeffrey Archer or Ruth Rendell. You're just Charles Rowan and a very different kettle of fish, believe me."

"All right, all right," he said. "I'm sorry. I should never have said what I said. I apologise. I didn't mean it."

"You're sure of that?"

"Sure, I'm sure."

"And you still want me to act for you?"

"Of course."

"And you'll do the Simon Cathcart show?"

He saw how he had been manipulated. The anger had all been put on. She had outmanoeuvred him and worked him into a corner. She was smart, no doubt about that. There was no way out for him now. He gave a sigh of resignation.

"Yes, I'll do it."

The anger had gone from her face like a passing summer storm. Now again all was serenity and light.

"I knew you would when you came to think about it," she said. "And you'll love it; really you will."

He doubted that. He doubted it very much indeed.

*

The chat show was called 'Simon Cathcart Presents' and it came on the air at prime viewing time on the Monday, though it was recorded in front of what was known as a live audience in the afternoon. Someone had dropped out of the original line-up and Ursula had been able to get Rowan in at short notice. He was not even a first choice; he was a stop-gap.

It started badly and got worse. Simon Cathcart, who was dressed in what appeared to be an electric blue satin suit, with a yellow tie, was in Rowan's opinion an even more loathsome character when seen in the flesh than when viewed on the television screen. He began by introducing Rowan as "Charlie Rowan, the crime novelist who finds the bodies of nude females in his oven." When the applause had died down he added: "We should all be so lucky." And was rewarded with a burst of inane laughter while Rowan squirmed.

Before bringing him on Cathcart had presented an American Country and Western singer named Margie Butterworth, a honey blonde in a fringed suede skirt and a matching jacket and tooled leather cowboy boots, who was in England to take part in an open-air concert at Wembley Stadium. She and Cathcart had traded badinage of a pretty earthy kind, and she had been followed by a man whose chief claim to rub shoulders with the rich and famous appeared to be the ability to play a mouth-organ with his nose, an accomplishment which with very little prompting he had proceeded to demonstrate.

Following as he did these two acts, Rowan could only wonder why he had allowed Ursula to coerce him into agreeing to become part of such a circus. The publicity was certainly not worth it; and from the moment Cathcart introduced him, not as Charles but as Charlie, it became obvious that the man's intention was to milk the interview for cheap laughs and make him look a fool. It was acutely embarrassing, and there was no way he could put a stop to it except by getting up and walking off the stage. He thought of doing so, but got no further than thinking. Instead, he remained there as if mesmerised, responding to Cathcart's prompting, hating it, hating the man, hating the audience, hating the lights and the camera crew and the whole damned set-up.

"And what are you working on at this moment, Charlie?" Cathcart asked. "A new magnum opus?"

He wanted to say: "No, you idiot; at this moment I'm not working on anything. I'm sitting here in front of a crowd of giggling morons answering bloody stupid questions from the biggest moron of the lot. And now I'm leaving. Goodbye."

But he did not. He stayed where he was and answered the question as lucidly and coolly as he could.

"So," Cathcart said, "this real murder business is making it difficult for you to concentrate on the fictional murders?"

"Yes."

"Seems to me that what you need, Charlie, is inspiration. Maybe you should take another look inside that oven. Might find something there, if only a bun."

Laughter at that! Top class wit! Moron talking; morons laughing! Get me out of here somebody! For God's sake get me out!

At last Cathcart was standing up. He was standing too.

"Thank you, Charlie Rowan," Cathcart said. And turning to the audience: "How about a big hand for Charlie."

Well, maybe it could have been worse. He could have said: "Clap hands, here comes Charlie."

And maybe he would if he had had the brains to think of it.

*

"How did it go?" Julia asked.

"It was murder," Rowan said.

After the recording he had gone straight back to her place, which was an old house in a quiet backwater, not far from Highgate Wood. A former owner, also an artist, had turned the attics into a studio with a wide expanse of window providing a north light. There was a walled garden at the back, with a lot of rampant rambler roses and a dilapidated summer-house and a sundial on a marble pedestal overgrown with ivy. Julia was no gardener and just let things grow wild. She said that way you made a sanctuary for birds and a host of butterflies in the summer. French windows opened on to this garden, and there was a bit of terrace with deckchairs and some urns and a plaster Cupid with a broken bow. It was hard to imagine that this was a part of Greater London.

"As bad as that?"

"Worse. I should never have done it. I should never have let myself be shunted into it."

"Well, of course Ursula can be very persuasive, can't she? Especially where you are concerned."

The remark was a trifle barbed, but he ignored it. "That man is an absolute swine. Do you know, he actually introduced me as Charlie Rowan. Can you imagine anyone introducing Dickens as Charlie Dickens?"

"Perhaps he would, if Dickens were alive and agreed to appear on his show."

"I shouldn't be at all surprised. He's got nerve enough for anything. I was preceded by a man playing a mouthorgan with his nose, of all things."

"Really? That I have to see. I'll watch it this evening and see if it's as bad as you say it is."

"I'd rather you didn't."

"But you'll want my opinion, won't you? And besides, I wouldn't miss it for worlds."

*

He was on his way back to the cottage long before 'Simon Cathcart Presents' came on the air. He was home in time to have watched it himself if he had wished to do so; but he did not. He knew the experience would have been excruciating.

Julia came through on the telephone soon after the show was timed to end. She made no attempt to spare him by hiding her honest opinion of it.

"You were right," she said. "It was dreadful. It made me cringe for you. How you stuck it out I can't imagine. In your place I'd have crowned the bastard with a microphone or something."

"I felt like doing it, but I resisted the temptation with iron self-control."

"I wish I could praise you for that, but I can't. It would have been the honourable thing to do."

"He would have sued me for assault."

"Quite possibly. Well, I hope it sells some books for you, because otherwise it'll be a dead loss."

"In my opinion that's what it is anyway. At least I've learnt my lesson. Never again."

"Once bitten, eh?"

"You've said it."

*

He had scarcely finished talking to Julia when the telephone rang again. This time it was Ursula.

"Congratulations," she said.

"On what?"

"The TV appearance of course. What else?"

"You mean you liked it?"

"I thought it was fine. Just the thing to put you in the public eye."

"It didn't strike you that I made a complete idiot of myself? Or rather that Cathcart did it for me."

"Not at all. Whatever gave you that idea?"

He wondered whether she had been watching the same programme as Julia. She seemed to have gained a completely different impression of it.

"He called me Charlie. Did you notice that? So now maybe there'll be crowds of people flocking to the bookshops and asking for novels by Charlie Rowan. Or more likely they won't be flocking at all."

"I can see you're in a filthy mood," she said. "It wasn't nearly as bad as you seem to imagine, I assure you. In fact you came over rather well. There was something very solid and honest about you. Very English."

"I am English. Or hadn't you noticed?"

"I had, as a matter of fact. And of course it's typically English to run oneself down. Foreigners don't do that. It's a thoroughly bad trait. You ought to kick the habit."

"Maybe I'll try. What would you like me to do? Should I go around in a T-shirt with 'I am Charles Rowan! I am the greatest!' printed on the front?"

"Now you're being silly. Incidentally, how is the new novel coming along?"

"You heard what I told Cathcart. It was the truth. I can't get anything done with all this other business going on. It's far too distracting."

"Don't worry, Charles. Let it simmer for a while; there's no need to hurry. Things will calm down and then you'll be able to go back to it."

"By that time I'll have lost the thread. Right now I feel inclined to scrap the damned thing."

"No, no, no. Don't do that. You're feeling depressed, but you'll get over it. You've had these barren patches before; they're inevitable. None of us can be at our best all the time."

"Not even you?"

"Not even me."

"You're at it again, aren't you?"

"At what again?"

"Giving me the treatment. Picking me up off the floor and dusting me down."

"It's what I'm here for," she said. "Amongst other things. And Charles —"

"Yes, Ursula?"

"In my book you are the greatest."

He wondered whether she was telling the truth or whether it was just more of the treatment, but he could not ask because she had rung off.

*

Hogan came on the line a good deal later. In fact it was getting on for midnight. Perhaps he thought he would wake Rowan from his beauty sleep; but if so he was unsuccessful; Rowan had not gone to bed. As soon as he heard Hogan's voice he switched on the recorder to get it on tape.

"I saw you on the box," Hogan said. "So you decided to make use of the publicity I've given you. Are you going to thank me?"

Rowan noticed a change in Hogan's tone; it had a certain jeering quality now, as though he were taunting the novelist, no longer bothering to keep up the pretence that his object was to help him.

"Why should I thank you for making it impossible for me to get on with my work?"

"Ah, that's what you told that clown, Simon Cathcart, wasn't it? Too bad. Maybe you'd like to get rid of me now. Maybe you'd rather I didn't pester you any more. Am I right?"

"You can be sure of that," Rowan said. "I wish I'd never heard your damned voice. Now all I ask of you is that you go away and leave me alone."

"But I can't do that, Charlie boy. You're my link man; my go-between. You're the one I have to talk to. In a way you might say we're partners. We have a lot in common, you and me."

"I can't think of a single thing I have in common with you," Rowan said.

"No? Well, perhaps you can't. Not yet. But you will, I promise you. Oh yes, you will."

Rowan had no idea what the man was talking about. It seemed to make no sense at all. He said:

"What made you pick on me?"

"You don't think it was just chance? A list of names and a pin maybe."

"I'm sure it wasn't. You may be mad, but there's method in your madness. I've no doubt about that."

"So you think I'm mad?"

"Yes."

"Don't kid yourself. I'm as sane as you are."

"Wrong. You're the one that's kidding himself, Hogan. You may not even know it yourself; you may think you're sane; but you're not. You're round the bend, pal; mad as a hatter."

"No!" Hogan's voice had risen in pitch, and Rowan could tell that he pierced the man's guard and scored a hit. Hogan was sensitive to that accusation of madness. "Don't say that."

"Why? Can't you take the truth? Does it bother you? Of course I can see why it might. You could end up in Broadmoor, you know. And that's not a pleasant prospect."

"It is not a prospect that bothers me," Hogan said. He had regained control over himself after losing it for a moment. "It will not happen."

"Look," Rowan said, "why don't you give yourself up and save yourself and everyone else a whole load of trouble? That would prove you really are sane."

Hogan laughed derisively. "Not at all. It would prove the exact opposite. I'm not as stupid as that, believe me. You can tell Chief Superintendent Dwyer and Chief Inspector Wint that when you see them again. I'm too smart for them, you know. Plodding flatfoot policemen with brains in their boots."

There was one thing about Hogan, Rowan thought: he had a pretty high opinion of himself; no doubt about that. But perhaps in the end he would be a little too smart for his own good. Eventually he might overreach himself and come an awful cropper. And it could not happen too soon.

"So you mean to go on with this game? This deadly game."

"Oh," Hogan said, "you can be sure of that. I haven't finished with you yet, Charlie. Cathcart called you that, didn't he? I'll wager you didn't like it. Made you squirm, didn't it? I can see why it would. It's not the name on the book jackets, is it? Charlie Rowan doesn't have quite the same ring to it as Charles Rowan; not the same author at all. In a way it belittles you."

He was perceptive enough to realise that. He could have imagined himself in Rowan's shoes and understood how that misuse of the name under which he wrote could irk an author. And he was not averse to rubbing a little salt in the wound.

So who the devil was he with an insight into the working of an author's mind?

Another writer?

Josh Froggatt?

He had been down that road before and it had taken him nowhere. So why not ask Hogan? He was the one who knew. The only one.

"Who are you? Who in hell are you?"

"I'm Hogan. And I'm not in hell — yet. I'll be in touch."

He rang off.

*

Rowan wondered whether to ring up the police at Wingstead and report that Hogan had been in contact again. But it was late and he could see no way it was going to make much difference if he postponed reporting the fact until the morning. So he decided to do just that. He had had a pretty full and tiring day and all he wanted to do now was to go to bed and have a good night's sleep.

He just hoped he would not dream about Hogan and more corpses. But in the event he did.

Chapter Nine – Old Man of the Sea

"YOU should have let us know at once," Wint said.

"It was nearly midnight when he rang up," Rowan explained. "What could you have done at that time of night?"

"Never mind what we could have done. It's the principle. If he rings again get through to us immediately, no matter what time it is."

Detective Chief Inspector Wint had himself driven out to Flint Cottage to pick up the tape of Rowan's conversation with Hogan. It was something that a constable could have done, so Rowan concluded that the chief inspector wanted to have a talk with him. And he was soon left in no doubt that Wint was not altogether pleased with his conduct. He had not himself seen the Simon Cathcart show, but he had heard about it and had not approved.

"I think it was very ill-advised, sir."

"I agree with you," Rowan said. "I wasn't in favour of it from the start, but I was persuaded to do it."

"Who by?"

"My agent."

"Your agent, eh? And I suppose the object was to get some free publicity that would help to sell your books?"

"That was her idea."

"Oh, it's a her, is it? And I don't suppose it occurred to either of you to consult with us before going ahead with the interview. You didn't think we would be interested, maybe?"

Rowan felt slightly embarrassed. Now that the chief inspector mentioned it, he could see that it would have been advisable to give the investigating team warning of the proposed television appearance, and even to seek approval of the project. It would have been the courteous thing to do, if nothing else.

"I'm sorry," he said. "You're quite right of course. You should have been consulted. I'm afraid I simply didn't think of it."

Wint accepted the apology rather grumpily. "Well, it's done now. But another time —"

"There won't be another time, you can count on that. One experience of that kind is more than enough for me. Anyway, I don't see how it can have done any harm to the investigation."

"Maybe it hasn't. But it isn't right, making entertainment of a murder. Not in my opinion, it isn't. You may think different. It's the way you make your living."

"Not from real murder. What I write is purely fictional."

"And I suppose that makes it all right?"

"I see nothing wrong in it."

Wint did not bother to argue the point; he had already aired his views on the subject. He said:

"Did Hogan watch the show?"

"Yes. That's what he rang up about. It's all on the tape."

"Did he say anything about future killings?"

"Nothing specific. Only that he hasn't finished yet. He clearly intends killing again."

"I should have been surprised if he didn't," Wint said. "He's not going to stop until we stop him."

"How is the investigation going? Any progress?"

Wint had to admit that there had been very little. "We've interviewed dozens of Range Rover owners, but none of them admits to having been near the Lazar House. It's believable. Low Lane is hardly what you'd call a busy highway. And we're hampered a bit by not knowing the exact day when Zak Smith says he saw the car. Frankly, I wouldn't put him down as the most reliable of witnesses, and he was probably half pissed at the time."

"You think he could have imagined it?"

"Oh no, I wouldn't go as far as that. But it doesn't really help us a lot. We need something more concrete, and at the moment nothing's coming up."

*

Rowan put a call through to Highgate, just to let Julia know the latest news about Hogan.

"It's spooky," she said. "I mean he seems to know everything about you, and you know nothing about him."

"Except that he's a murderer with some kind of bee in his bonnet, and possibly drives a Range Rover. Do you know anybody who does that among your acquaintances?"

"No, I don't. It's mostly the country set, isn't it? Tweeds and Barbour jackets and green wellies and all that."

"Like Major Parkin, for instance?"

"Well, yes. Though of course I haven't met him, so I don't really know what he's like."

"You haven't missed much. I don't think you'd like him. He does drive a Range Rover, but the police seem to have crossed him off their list of suspects. Not that they have a list, as far as I can tell. They're baffled. They're like Mr Micawber, waiting for something to turn up."

"And that something could be another dead body."

"Too true. Anyway, if you're right what they should be looking for is a country gentlemen or a farmer or suchlike. But somehow I have a feeling he isn't one of that brigade."

"Why?"

"No good reason. Just a hunch."

"Hunches aren't evidence, are they?"

"No. Are you still planning to come down here next weekend?"

"Nothing's happened to make me change my mind. You want me to, don't you?"

"Of course. I just thought that with this nut-case hanging around, you might feel safer in London."

"Oh, rubbish. Where could I be safer than with you? Besides, we have no reason to believe he has me in his sights, have we?"

Rowan reflected that it was she who had first suggested this possibility. But perhaps on second thoughts she had seen how unlikely it was.

"I'll be seeing you then."

*

Wint rang up to tell him what conclusion the expert had drawn from the tape.

"He says there's no doubt that the voice is disguised. His opinion is that the man is better class than he's trying to give the impression of being. The accent is not identifiable with any particular region; it's just coarsened to mislead you."

"Which is about what I thought."

"There's something else. Our man detects a taunting quality in what Hogan said to you."

"Well, I noticed that too."

"But when he first got in touch with you he was offering to help and you thought he was friendly, didn't you?"

"Yes."

"That's all gone now. It was almost certainly a pose. Now he's no longer bothering to conceal his true nature. He probably hates you; that's what our man says. He's convinced it was no chance thing that Hogan picked you for his confidant after killing the woman. It was all planned from the start. We think he's building up to something, and that something could be killing you, Mr Rowan. You're the ultimate victim, but how many steps it will take him to get to you is anybody's guess. That's the conclusion we've come to."

"Well, thanks for telling me," Rowan said. "Now you really have put my mind at ease."

"I know it's not nice," Wint said, "but it's best you should know. If you're forewarned you can take precautions."

"But I don't get a bodyguard?"

"I'm afraid not. We haven't got the manpower. And there's no telling how long it would have to last. It's not even as if we knew for certain that your life is in danger. This is only conjecture after all."

"But you think the conjecture is right?"

"Yes, we do."

"Chief Inspector, you've made my day."

"And there's another thing our man gathered from the tape: Hogan has a great sense of his own superiority. He even said he was too smart for us, didn't he?"

Rowan remembered what Hogan had said about Dwyer and Wint — plodding flatfoot policemen with brains in their boots. That would not have gone down too well with the gentlemen named, even if it might have provided some amusement for the lower ranks.

"He may even think he's above the law; but one day he'll find he isn't. We'll get him eventually, Mr Rowan; never fear."

Which was not quite what he had said on a previous occasion, as Rowan recalled. And anyway, eventually could be far into the future, and meanwhile he was in the firing line. At least, that seemed to be the general opinion. And it was not one that he could feel at all happy about.

*

On the Wednesday Josh Froggatt delivered a parcel of books which Rowan had ordered. He too had seen the Simon Cathcart show and thought Cathcart had been far too familiar.

"He ought to have treated you with more respect, Mr Rowan. You're a topnotch writer, you are, and what is he but a jumped-up little TV interviewer. People like him, they get to thinking they're something special, but they're not. It's all that money they're paid. Goes to their heads, that's what it does."

Rowan listened to Froggatt's voice and tried to compare it in his mind with Hogan's; but he could detect no similarity. And if the expert had been right in surmising that Hogan's accent was a disguised upper class one, that certainly ruled out Josh Froggatt. But experts could be as wrong as the next person.

Before leaving Froggatt produced two typescripts, each neatly stapled. "A couple of short stories I'd like you to give an opinion on, Mr Rowan, if you're not too busy to read them. Seeing as how you can't seem to get on with that novel you're writing, I thought you might be able to spare the time."

Rowan wondered whether Froggatt was indulging in a bit of subtle mockery, but there was no indication of it in his guileless face. He took the typescripts and promised to read them.

When Froggatt had gone he cursed himself for so easily yielding once again to this kind of imposition. Reading the stories, which were lurid if not entirely grammatical, was the chief event of his day.

*

Hogan rang up quite early on the Thursday morning. Rowan had breakfasted on muesli and coffee and was making a half-hearted attempt to sort out the confusion on his desk. The notebook, open at an almost completed page 84, seemed to rebuke him for his lack of progress. Somehow he had entirely lost his grasp of the story line, and the characters in the novel had become blurred in his mind. He wondered whether Froggatt ever suffered from writer's block.

Hogan came straight to the point with no beating about the bush.

"I've got another one for you, Charlie."

Rowan's heart sank. He did not have to ask what Hogan was referring to: 'another one' could mean only one thing.

"Damn you!" he said. "Damn you, Hogan!"

He heard the man's throaty chuckle. "Now don't take it like that, Charlie. This is what makes life interesting for you. You might get bored otherwise. I'm saving you from that — the dread ennui, eh? You should be grateful."

"Damn you, Hogan!" Rowan said again. "You know what you're doing to me, don't you? All that talk at first of helping me was just eyewash. You're plaguing me and you know it. It's what you intended doing right from the start, isn't it?"

"Is that what you think?"

"It's what I know. Are you going to deny it?"

"Why should I deny it?" Hogan spoke nonchalantly, as though it were a matter of supreme indifference to him. "You think what you like; it's all one to me."

"And you're not going to get off my back?"

"Oh, no. I'm the Old Man of the Sea. You'll never shake me off till your dying day, and you'd better resign yourself to that."

It was a promise full of ill omen, a more direct intimation of his ultimate design than he had ever given before. Rowan could not be unaware of this and it gave him no ease of mind.

"Why, Hogan? Just tell me why."

"You'll know one day. Then all will be revealed with blinding clarity. But not yet. The game has to be played out."

"And you make the rules?"

"Naturally. It's my game after all. And now don't you want to know where it is this time? You haven't asked."

"I don't have to. You'll tell me anyway."

"Yes, of course. So I'll give you a clue like I did the first time. A humped-back bridge."

There was the usual rattling sound before the line went dead. Hogan had said his latest piece and was no doubt well satisfied with it.

Chapter Ten – Not Really Happy

ROWAN put down the telephone and realised that he had forgotten to switch on the recorder. Well, it made no difference; there would have been nothing on the tape to give any more help in tracking Hogan down than the other one had. Which was practically none at all.

The clue was an easy one. The hump-backed bridge was almost certainly the one in Low Lane near the Lazar House. And if Hogan had left a body there it was very audacious of him to choose a spot so close to the place where he had dumped the first one. But in fact he would have run very little risk if he had gone there in the night; the police had seen no point in keeping a watch on the lane, since it would have appeared to them so unlikely that Hogan would do what in the event he had indeed done.

Always supposing that this was not a hoax, a way of teasing both him and the police, of keeping them on their toes and chasing wild geese. But he did not believe it was a hoax, though this was a possibility. When Hogan had given a pointer before it had led to a dead body, and the likelihood was that this one would do so too.

He thought of going to the bridge to check up before calling in the police, but remembering Wint's instructions to get onto them immediately if Hogan rang again, he decided to do just that.

Wint himself was not at the incident room in Wingstead police-station, but the message was taken by Detective Constable Ryder, and that was enough to set the ball rolling.

"Have you been to the bridge?" Ryder asked.

"No. I've only just had the call from Hogan."

"Good. Don't touch anything. I'll be there very shortly."

Rowan drove to Low Lane and parked his car well short of the hump-backed bridge. No one else had yet arrived and the lane was deserted. It all seemed very peaceful and it was hard to imagine that such a charming country scene could perhaps conceal the evidence of a gruesome crime.

He walked to the bridge and looked over the parapet on each side, but could see no sign of any body. There had been several weeks of dry weather and the stream had become little more than a trickle. Shingle was visible in the bed on one side and on the other the marshy ground had dried out to such an extent that the muddy stems and even the roots of some of the rushes and other water weeds could be plainly seen. From this marsh an odour of rotting vegetation and noisome mud was wafted to the nostrils, and a pair of moorhens dashed away as they became aware of human presence.

Ryder arrived within a few minutes. He also left his car some distance away and walked to the bridge. He was carrying something in his hand, and when he drew closer Rowan could see that it was a mirror on an extending rod.

"Have you spotted a body?" Ryder asked.

"No, nothing."

"If it's here it's likely under the bridge. He wouldn't leave it in the open for anyone to see. That's not his way. I'll take a look."

He went to the parapet on the marshy side and lowered the mirror nearly to the level of the stream.

"Yes," he said, "it's there all right. He wasn't kidding you."

"I didn't think he was."

"Want to see it?"

Rowan was not at all sure that he did, but he accepted the invitation. He leaned over the parapet and looked in the mirror. He could see the body lying under the arch of the bridge; a naked woman only half submerged in the shallow stream which gurgled past her, fanning out the long blonde hair like trailing water weed.

"The bastard!"

Ryder glanced at him. "You're talking about Hogan?"

"Who else would I be talking about? He's the one who put her there, isn't he?"

On this side of the bridge the bank sloped gently down to the edge of the water, and it was no doubt the way that Hogan had carried the body. There were no footprints in the soft muddy ground, but the soil had been disturbed as if by a garden fork or a rake. Ryder pointed this out.

"He's clever; you have to give him that. Covers his tracks. Well, I'd better report back that we've found the body."

He returned to his car, and Rowan could see him using the telephone in it. Soon they would all be here, the whole damned circus: detectives, doctor, photographers, fingerprint men, the lot. And who was this one?

Another nobody? Another unidentifiable piece of human flesh from which the spirit had departed, never to return?

He had no great desire to remain there, hanging around on the fringes of the action while the professionals did their various jobs; but he supposed he would be expected to. Wint would certainly wish to question him; though what was there to tell? That Hogan had rung up and told him there was another one for him? That Hogan had sounded cheerful? None of this would advance the investigation by as much as an inch.

*

"You've got the tape of the conversation, I suppose?" Wint said.

"Well, no," Rowan admitted. "I forgot to switch on the machine. So I'm afraid there's nothing."

Wint was not pleased; he could see that.

"We look to you for co-operation, Mr Rowan. It doesn't help us when you choose to ignore instructions."

"I didn't choose to. I simply forgot."

Wint gave him a look which seemed to hint that in his opinion people ought not to forget things like that.

*

The woman appeared to be somewhat older than the first one, but she had been killed by the same method, a ligature round the neck, possibly a thin cord. Again the ligature could not be found. Again no fingerprints had been left anywhere near. So they were really no closer to solving the puzzle, because this victim too would probably not be identified. A photograph of the dead face would be published so that anyone who recognised it might come forward; but that had been tried with the other one with no result. Somebody surely must have known her, but either they had not seen the picture or had not been prepared to have anything to do with the police.

Wint had not been altogether surprised; his opinion was that the woman had not come from anywhere in the vicinity but from further afield. He also believed she was not the sort who would be living with her family. She had probably left them years ago; maybe had been brought up in an institution and had gone in for the more questionable ways of earning a living, associating with the kind of people who regarded the upholders of the law as enemies rather than friends. Such people might be extremely reluctant to become involved.

"And even if we knew who these women were," Wint said, "it might not help us to find the killer. His contact with them could have started and ended the same night. They were probably complete strangers to him, and he to them."

"It sounds to me," Rowan said, "as if what you're suggesting is that they were prostitutes."

"It would not surprise me in the least."

The possibility had already occurred to Rowan. "In that case I suppose he could be the kind of nutter who has some grudge against women of that sort and feels impelled to rid the world of as many of them as he possibly can."

"Oh," Wint said, "I agree that he's almost certainly a nutter, but not that kind. He's just using the whores for a purpose."

"You mean to harass me?"

"Exactly. You're still the key to this business, Mr Rowan. I mean to say, if his object was simply to kill these women, why would he go to the bother of hiding the bodies and then telling you where to find them? It wouldn't make sense."

Rowan had known this already. Hogan himself had practically admitted as much. Wint was merely confirming the fact, and it was no use looking for any reassurance from that quarter.

"You can't think of anyone who might want to do this to you?" Wint asked. "An enemy of some sort."

"As far as I know I have no enemies."

Wint shook his head sadly. "I guess we all have a few of them if we only knew. And you certainly have one."

*

Rowan got on the telephone to Julia as soon as he could. He wanted to tell her about the latest development before she heard the news from some other source. She was appalled.

"It's dreadful. Oh God, Charles, is there no way of stopping the man?"

"Not until we know who he is. And that at present seems to be beyond the capacity of the police to discover."

"But why does this man Hogan tell you about the killing? What is his object?"

"I don't know," Rowan said. He thought it best not to tell her that the police now regarded him as the ultimate victim and that it was all leading up to this. It would only have added to her worry, and she was worried enough already. He too, for that matter. "You're coming down here tomorrow as planned, are you?"

"Yes, of course."

He wondered whether to try to persuade her to stay at her home until this Hogan business was finished. He wanted to keep her away from that madman at all costs. But who could tell when it would be finished — and in what way? And if he insisted he might only succeed in making her even more alarmed than she was already. And she would probably come anyway.

"Well, at least you should miss the press gang. They're gathering already. This is meat and drink to them."

*

He was right about that. They arrived in the afternoon, and he had to face the questioning again. The discovery of a second body made the whole affair even more fascinating. Already there were hints of a serial killer at large, though whether just two instalments added up to a serial was questionable.

His own connection with the crimes was subject now to even closer scrutiny. It was inevitable, of course; they sensed a mystery and believed he was holding out on them; that he must know more than he would admit.

"This guy who rings you up, Mr Rowan. You still don't know his name?"

"No."

"He hasn't told you?"

"Would he be stupid enough to do that?"

"But you must call him something."

"I do. I call him a bastard."

One of the women reporters wanted to know where the girlfriend was. "Julia Spence. Isn't that her name?"

"Yes, it is. And she's not here right now."

"You split up?"

"No, we didn't split up. She has her own place in London; it's where her studio is. That's where she is. Working."

He regretted immediately having told them that. There had been no need to reveal so much, but things just slipped out if you failed to take care. The tongue seemed to take over.

"Whereabouts in London?" the reporter asked. She was young but no beauty. She had mousy hair and a pointed nose which seemed to peck away at him as she asked the questions.

"Never mind where," Rowan said.

"You're not telling?"

"No, I'm not telling."

It made no difference. If they really wanted to know Julia's address they already knew enough about her to ferret it out. But maybe they would not take the trouble.

"Do you think she's in danger?"

"Why should she be in danger?"

"She could be the next on the list."

"I see no reason why she should be. Do you?"

"She's a woman. The killer seems to go for women, doesn't he?"

"Well, for God's sake! Half the adult population are women."

"But he doesn't have any links with half the adult population."

"He doesn't have any link with Miss Spence either."

"Oh, but that isn't true, is it? I mean you're the link, aren't you?"

He refused to answer that one. Because she was right, of course; he could not deny it. And it was already bothering him; he had not needed the suggestion of this damned female newspaper scribe to alert him to the possible danger. True, there was no obvious reason why Hogan should turn his attention to Julia; but did a man like that need to have any reason?

"How's the new book coming along?" one of the gang asked.

He declined to answer that one too.

*

She arrived the next day in her white Mini, and he was delighted to see her — as always. He had heard the car and had the door of the cottage open as she reached the threshold. She hugged him impulsively, and he was glad the press gang was no longer there, because it was quite an emotional moment — and a private one.

Later they talked. She wanted to know all the details that he had not given her on the telephone, and he told her about Wint's theory that the women were prostitutes.

"But there's no proof of that, is there?"

"No proof. But it seems likely."

"Well," she said, after giving it some thought, "if that's the case; if Hogan is just going for that class of victim, you and I are safe enough, aren't we? It's not our profession." She gave a laugh, but he thought it was an uneasy one, and he decided not to tell her the rest of what Wint had said, because that was not so reassuring.

"Has he called you again?" she asked.

"Hogan? No, he hasn't."

It surprised him a little; he would have expected the man to ring up and gloat; do some more of the taunting. But there had been nothing; for the present it seemed that Hogan had decided to lie low and let things ride. Perhaps he was recharging his batteries in preparation for the next move.

Ursula had rung up. She had heard or read about the latest murder and wanted to know how he was taking it.

"You really are keeping yourself in the news, aren't you, Charles?"

"Wrong," he said. "I'm being kept in the news; which is a very different thing. My role in all this is entirely passive."

"Well, active or passive, the result is the same: publicity."

"Damn publicity. And if you're thinking of getting me on another chat show, forget it. I'm not doing that again."

"I'm not asking you to. I doubt whether Simon would want to do a follow-up anyway."

"I'm glad to hear it."

"But it is a funny old business, isn't it? This man picking on you for a confidant, I mean. What's driving him?"

"I've no idea what's driving him, and frankly I don't find it the least bit funny."

"No," she said, "I don't suppose you would. Really."

*

They were in bed when Julia revealed that there was another matter on her mind besides the killings.

"There's something I think I should tell you," she said. "I had a visit from Peter the other day."

"From Dacre! What did he want?"

"To talk. At first I was in half a mind not to let him in, but he seemed very subdued, not at all like his usual arrogant self, and I couldn't see how it would do any harm to talk, so I agreed."

"What did he want to talk about?"

"You and me and him."

"The devil he did!"

"He'd been abroad, you see; just come back from Brazil actually. He arrived in England the day when the first killing hit the headlines. And then apparently he saw you on the Simon Cathcart show, and it worried him; you being mixed up in something like that."

"He was worried for me? I find that hard to believe."

"Well, not really you particularly; it was for my sake actually. He said he thought I might be in danger, and besides, it was pretty unpleasant for me even without the threat to my life. He said this unknown murderer might strike again, and probably would."

"He was on the mark there. I take it that this visit took place before the second killing?"

"Yes. It was Tuesday as a matter of fact."

"You didn't mention it on the phone."

"I couldn't make up my mind whether to or not. I was afraid it might make you angry."

"But you've decided to take that risk now."

"Yes. I've been thinking it over, and it seemed best."

"And there's a bit more to it, isn't there?"

"Yes, there is. He asked me to break things off with you and go back to him."

"He's got a bloody nerve. You told him it was no go, of course?"

"Yes. But it wasn't easy to get rid of him. He was actually pleading with me; something I can't remember him ever doing before. He said I'd be safe with him and there was no telling what might happen to me if I stayed with you, because the unknown killer seemed to have a thing about women and I was obviously at risk from being so close to you. I had to be very firm with him, and in the end I managed to convince him it wasn't on."

"How did he take it?"

"Not too well. I thought for a moment he was going back to the old way and fly off the handle. But he controlled himself, though it must have been an effort. He just said very quietly. 'I hope you don't live to regret this'. And then he said goodbye and left. I even felt the weeniest bit sorry for him."

"No need to," Rowan said. "Can't you see how it was? He comes back from abroad and the first thing that catches his eye is this murder business. Well, he's a clever man and he sees a way he can use it to his own advantage. He makes out he's thinking only of your safety, but that's just eyewash of course; what he's really thinking about is none other than Mr

Peter Dacre and how he can make a profit by the situation. Oh, he's the smart one all right; he's got an eye to the main chance and no mistake."

She said thoughtfully: "It didn't seem like that at the time. He sounded very genuine."

"But of course he did. It was all part of the act. You do see that, don't you?"

"I suppose you could be right." She still sounded doubtful about it, as though only half convinced.

"You bet I could."

"And you're not angry?"

"Why should I be angry? You sent him packing. I've still got you, haven't I? And you're going to stick with me, aren't you?"

"Oh, yes." She snuggled up to him, warm and sweet-scented and utterly desirable. "Always."

"That's my girl," Rowan said.

But nevertheless, he was not so happy about that visit of Dacre's. No, not happy at all.

Chapter Eleven – Pick-up

MAJOR Edward Millhouse Parkin drove up to London in his Range Rover and arrived in the early morning. He had a meal in the dining-room of a quiet hotel in Kensington where he was in the habit of staying whenever he spent some time in the Metropolis, and where he was well-known to the staff. But he was careful not to consume more than the smallest quantity of light wine, and he did not linger at the table.

He took the Range Rover from the car-park where he had left it and drove to an area not far from Liverpool Street Station. Here he picked up a prostitute; a young woman, probably little more than twenty years of age, not unattractive and with a good figure. Parkin had a discerning eye and had chosen this one from a number who were plying their trade in the light of the street-lamps. She took a close look at him, was apparently satisfied with what she saw and stated her price. Parkin did not quibble, and she got into the vehicle and seated herself beside him, closing the door behind her.

He drove only a short distance to a quiet side-street and stopped the car.

"I have a proposition to make to you," he said.

"What kind of proposition?" She was immediately suspicious. "Something kinky, is it?"

"Not in the sense I imagine you mean," Parkin said. "What is your name?"

"Jackie."

"Well, Jackie, how would you like to earn quite a lot of money with very little trouble?"

"How much?"

"One thousand pounds."

She stared at him. She was a blonde, hair down to her shoulders, round-faced, blue-eyed, with pouting lips. The faded denim skirt she was wearing was tight and very short; it scarcely reached to the tops of her thighs when she was sitting down. The legs were long, and sturdy rather than slender. She might have made a good runner if athletics had been her game; which it was not. Her breasts were firm under the stretched T-shirt with the face of Che Guevara imprinted on it.

Parkin noticed all this with satisfaction. She would do splendidly. Always supposing she was amenable and did not raise any stupid objections. He wanted no one who would make trouble for him; he liked things to go smoothly.

"A grand," she said. "For that money it has to be something really wild."

"I wouldn't say so. It's quite simple. I wish you to play a part."

"Acting, you mean?"

"In a way, yes."

"Look, mister," she said. "I don't know what you take me for, but I'm no bloody actress, You don't pick up that sort in the streets."

Parkin smiled. With someone like this you had to be patient; you had to spell it out to them a bit at a time, overcoming a natural suspicion of any unusual proposal.

"It will be perfectly easy. You will have no lines to learn; you will not even have to speak."

"So what do I have to do?"

"You have to take part in a kind of ceremony."

"Here," she said, grinning suddenly, "you're not wanting me to do a Lady Godiva, riding naked on a white horse? I ain't never been on a horse. Don't know as I could stay on."

"You don't have to. It's not that. It's quite a different kind of ceremony and will take place at night."

"And where will it be?"

"In the country. You will stay at my house for the night, possibly two nights. It will make a nice change for you."

"Oh, I'm sure. And then you bring me back here?"

"Yes, of course."

"You better gimme some idea of this here ceremony, so's I know what I'd be letting myself in for."

He told her.

"Sounds bloody stupid to me," she said. "But if that's what you want, it's okay, I reckon. Is it payment in advance?"

"Now, now," Parkin said, "you can't expect that. You might take the money and run."

"And how do I know you won't cheat me out of my fee when the job's finished?"

Parkin conceded that she had a point. "I suggest we do a compromise. Five hundred in advance, the other half on completion of contract. How does that sound to you?"

"Okay. Let's have it."

Parkin took a leather wallet from his pocket and counted out ten fifty-pound notes, which he handed to the girl.

"Now we'll be on our way."

"Harig on," she said. "If I'm going to be away for a couple of nights I'll need to take some gear. We'll have to go to my place first, so's I can pick it up."

Parkin shook his head. "That will not be necessary. You'll find everything you need at my house. You will not be the first lady who has stayed the night."

"Lady, is it? Oh my!"

*

It was even better than she had expected. The house was the kind she had seen only in glossy magazines or on the telly; she had never set foot inside such a fine old building. The front was floodlit by electric lamps situated on the edge of the gravelled forecourt, and if she had known more about architecture than she did she might have recognised it as being Georgian.

Major Parkin took her inside and informed her that there was no one else in the house.

"Mrs Summers, my housekeeper, who is also the cook, doesn't sleep here; she comes in daily, with the maid. One has to make do with that sort of arrangement these days. It used to be different; a place like this would have a host of servants. Of course I have a gardener-cum-handyman and a gardener's boy, and there are the estate workers too —"

"Oh," she said, "you have an estate."

"Of a sort, yes."

"Golly! You must be stinking rich."

He smiled faintly. "Is that what you think?"

"With all this! What else would I think? Aren't you?"

He admitted to being reasonably well off. "But taxes are a burden. One cannot live in the old style."

She had no idea what the old style was. She was impressed by the spacious entrance hall and the wide staircase curving away to the upper regions; it was like something out of a glittering film. When he conducted her to the bedroom which was to be hers for the night she was amazed; she could not have imagined that anything quite so grand would have been provided for her accommodation.

Parkin slid back the doors of a capacious wardrobe and revealed a wide selection of women's clothing. "You may take your pick. I imagine you'll find something to fit well enough. What you choose you can keep. Underclothes are in the drawers."

There was a mahogany dressing-table with three mirrors and a range of cosmetics. The bed was king-size, the draperies and wallpaper all of a bluish tint, harmonising with the thick pile carpet which gave her a feeling as of walking on air.

Parkin opened a door and revealed an en suite bathroom, gleaming under the electric light with gold plate and pale blue porcelain.

"Satisfactory?"

"Are you kidding?" she said. "It's super. Meanter say, gold taps and all. I never saw nothing like it. My!"

"I will leave you now," Parkin said. "I have some phone calls to make. Arrangements, you know. I have no doubt you will be able to amuse yourself for a time. Why not try the bath? There is plenty of hot water."

She wondered whether it was a hint that she was not quite as clean as he would have wished. But she did not take offence. He was paying the piper and had a right to call the tune.

*

She was in the bath when he appeared again. He walked into the bathroom without bothering to give as much as a tap on the door to warn her he was there. She had poured half a bottle of bath foam into the water as it was running from the tap, and it had frothed up to the brim. It had a scent of herbs and roses, and she was luxuriating in the warm slippery feel of it on her skin, nothing of her visible except her head with the blonde hair piled up in a knot on top.

She grinned at Parkin. "Well, come right in. Make yourself at home." She was beginning to lose any initial awe she might have had of this rather tubby little man with his ruddy cheeks and his receding ginger hair. Now he quite amused her. She wondered how old he was. In his fifties, she would have guessed. That was pretty old in her view, but she had found that men of that age were likely to be as randy as any of them. Perhaps they were terrified of losing it all. "Don't stand on ceremony."

He had not told her his name. When she had asked he had said sharply that it was no concern of hers. She had no idea either where this place was to which he had brought her. It had been dark all the way, and even in daylight she would probably not have been aware of where they were going; she had very little knowledge of the country beyond the borders of Greater London.

"Stand up," Parkin said.

She stared at him. "Do what?"

"Stand up. I want to see what you look like."

She stood up, bubbles clinging to her, skin glistening with moisture.

"Venus rising from the foam," Parkin murmured.

"What say?"

"Nothing. You wouldn't understand. Now step out on to the bath-mat."

She did this, limbs dripping, facing Parkin with arms akimbo and a mocking smile on her lips in a parody of seduction; a naiad parading her charms for a satyr's delectation.

He gazed at her for a full minute, his slightly protuberant eyes making a thorough examination of every aspect of her body, ordering her to turn so that he could have the rear view and then turn again to face him. She could feel the water cooling on her skin, the bubbles drying and subsiding. She would have liked to step back into the bath and steep herself in its voluptuous warmth, but he had given no sign that he had finished with her yet.

Then he sighed faintly and said: "Yes, you will do. You will do very nicely."

He turned and moved towards the door.

"Is that all?" she asked.

"Yes," he said, "that is all. For the present."

Thankfully she stepped back into the bath. He was certainly kinky, that one. But what the hell! For a thousand quid she could take a little kinkiness.

*

She was almost asleep when he came into the room and slipped into the bed beside her. She had half expected that he would but could not be certain.

"Do I get a bonus for this?" she asked. "It was not in the contract." But she was only kidding.

"I know of no contract," he said. "But you will have the clothes, and that is a bonus."

She felt his hands moving over her body, confirming by touch what his eyes had told him earlier. She could smell the whisky on his breath and sense the excitement in him.

"Jackie always seems to me an odd name for a girl," he said. "I suppose it is short for Jacqueline."

"Then you suppose wrong. I was christened Jackie."

"Is that so? In my book it's still a boy's name."

"Well, I'm no boy."

"That," he said, "I have already determined."

She wished he would get finished with the preliminaries and move on to the rest of it. She wanted to sleep. She was dog-tired. Or in her case should it be bitch-tired?

"How long have you been on the streets?" he asked.

"I was fourteen when I started." And what in hell did he want to know that for? It was none of his business.

"That's very young. Do you have any regrets?"

"No. I'd do it again. It's better than starving."

"Nobody starves in this country today."

It was easy for him to say that, but how did he know? And why in hell didn't he stop pawing her and cut the cackle and get on with it so that she could go to sleep?

*

He was gone when she woke in the morning. A dumpy girl had brought in a cup of tea on a tray, with a cup and a saucer and a jug of milk and a bowl of sugar. She drew back the curtains and let the daylight in.

"Who are you?" Jackie asked.

"I'm Maggie. Mrs Simmons told me to bring the tea."

"Oh, the housekeeper."

"Yes. And I was to ask if you'd like to have your breakfast in bed or would rather have it downstairs."

She thought about it. She could not remember when she had last had breakfast in bed. It was supposed to be a luxury, but it was overrated. In her opinion anyway. She decided against it.

"Tell Mrs Simmons I'll be getting up."

"There was a message from the major too. He's gone out and he won't be back until after lunch. He said you're to do what you like to pass the time. You can go for a walk round the estate, but don't get lost, he said."

So he was a major. A military man, if he was not in the Sally Army, and he certainly did not act like one of that lot. Come to think of it, he did have a certain military air about him in spite of the tubbiness and the baldness; and he spoke like a man who was used to giving orders. Well, it was a new experience for her, sleeping with an army officer. And there would be another new experience later. She was not sure she was going to enjoy it; in fact she felt a bit nervous about the whole idea; it would be rather like going on the stage for the first time. If she had been a stripper it would have been different, but she had never taken up that lark.

She found Mrs Simmons in the kitchen making pastry. The housekeeper was a plump middle-aged woman with pleasant enough features but no pretensions to beauty. She gave Jackie a friendly greeting.

"Ah, there you are, my dear. Found your way all right. Now what would you like? A proper old-fashioned English breakfast of bacon-and-egg and toast-and-marmalade? Or are you one of these here weight-watchers who just have half a grapefruit and a slice of rye bread?"

Jackie was wearing a pair of jeans and a green sweat shirt that she had found among the gear in the bedroom. She planned to take some of the other stuff when she left, whether she had worn it or not. She would just try it on for size first.

The time was already coming up to ten o'clock, and she decided to skip breakfast and settle for a cup of coffee and a biscuit.

"Whatever you say, dear." Mrs Simmons was prepared to be cooperative and appeared to accept Jackie without question as just a normal house guest.

Jackie drank the coffee and ate a digestive biscuit in the kitchen, sitting on a stool and chatting with Mrs Simmons, who told her that she came from a village called Little Madding and rode to work each day on a bicycle. She was married to a tractor-driver and had one son, who had left home and gone to work in Ipswich.

Jackie tried to get some information out of her about the major, but in that quarter Mrs Simmons was not forthcoming. It was apparent that her employer and his business were not subjects for discussion; at least not by her. Probably it was not at all unusual for the major to bring strange women into the house, and Mrs Simmons, like a good discreet servant, was willing to take them at face value and ask no awkward questions.

To pass the time before lunch, which was scheduled for one o'clock, Jackie followed the major's suggestion and went for a stroll in the grounds of the big house. She found the gardener and his young assistant at work in the flower garden and was given advice regarding which direction to take for the best views: The boy looked at her shyly and said nothing, but was obviously captivated by this gorgeous golden-haired creature who had suddenly appeared from nowhere to add a touch of glamour to the mundane scene.

Despite the warning given to her, she got lost in the woods and was late back for lunch. Mrs Simmons took it in good part.

"Not used to the country, are you, dear? Easy to lose your way where there's no street signs and no policemen to ask for directions. Ah well, here you are and no bones broken."

*

Major Parkin returned in the middle of the afternoon. Jackie was dozing on an extending chair on the terrace, and he came straight over to her.

"It's all fixed up."

"That's nice," she said, having no idea of what he had been doing to fix it up. He seemed, she thought, in a state of barely suppressed excitement, as though he were becoming keyed up to some great event. She knew, of course, what the event was to be, since she was to be a part of it and he had had to tell her. But she was surprised that its imminence should affect him in quite this way. Still, you never could tell what would turn people on; some reacted to one thing, some to another; and this was evidently the one for him.

"You've managed to amuse yourself?" he asked.

She doubted whether he was really interested, but she told him how she had passed the time. "You've got a lovely place here. You ain't half lucky."

Not that she would have wanted to live there. It was too quiet. It was all right for a while, but before long it would have driven her up the wall. She preferred the bright lights of London; the traffic and the people and all that.

"Lucky?" he said, as if it were an idea that had never occurred to him. "Is that what you think I am? Lucky."

"Looks like it to me. You got everything, ain't you? Big house, fine estate, money —"

"Money isn't everything." He spoke sharply, even a trifle angrily, it seemed.

"Maybe not. But I wouldn't mind having a bit more of it, and that's a fact."

"Be content with what you've got," he said. "That's the way to stay happy."

He turned abruptly and walked away. She watched him go. He was an odd one for sure.

*

Later she saw him carrying some gear out of the house and stowing it in the Range Rover. She strolled across to take a closer look.

"What's all that?"

"Props," he said. "Just props."

It didn't look like props to her. Props were things you used to hold clothes lines up, weren't they? You would never have got a prop in the back of a Range Rover.

*

It was late in the evening when the cars started arriving. Mrs Simmons and Maggie had long since gone home, as had the gardener and the boy. Jackie did not count the cars, but there were several of them. Both men and women came in them, and they assembled in the house and had drinks in the hall, standing around and chatting to one another like old friends.

Jackie stayed in the background. Parkin seemed to think it unnecessary to introduce her to these people, and she had no great desire to be introduced. They were the sort with whom she had nothing in common, speaking with voices that persuaded her to classify them in her mind as upper-class twits; though there were some with broader country accents who looked to her like farmers. Judging by the cars parked outside, none of the owners was short of the odd quid or two. There were no old bangers or anything of that sort among them.

It was getting on for half-past eleven when they moved off. Jackie rode with Parkin in the Range Rover. He led the way and the others followed.

Chapter Twelve – Ceremony

THE two boys came from Little Madding. Tommy Drake was twelve years old and Garry Mallet was just thirteen. They were riding bicycles and it was getting on for midnight. Each had managed to sneak out of his house without the knowledge of his parents. They were little daredevils, and the object of their nocturnal journey was to prove to two other boys of a similar age that they were not afraid to keep a midnight rendezvous in the graveyard of the old Little Madding church, which was on the Astley Manor estate.

The church had been disused for years and was gradually falling into decay, though the roof was still reasonably sound. It was slated, and had therefore not been a target of thieves, who would have stripped it of its covering if it had been lead. It was accessible by way of a narrow road though the surrounding trees, which, though partially overgrown, was still usable. For the boys' bicycles it was rough going, and the beams from their lamps shed a wavering light on the way ahead of them.

Neither was feeling especially daring at this hour of the night, knowing the kind of nightmarish character of the meeting-place to which they were heading; but it would have lowered their reputations among their peers if they had allowed the two rival boys to go there and discover that they had chickened out. So they pressed on and came suddenly on a number of cars parked just outside the low brick wall that enclosed the graveyard.

This was completely unexpected, and they dismounted and took stock of the situation. And then they noticed that there were lights in the church, and this was really not at all as it should have been.

"Ghosts!" Tommy whispered. "Let's get out of here."

But Garry was more logically minded. "Ghosts don't come in cars and don't carry lights. There's people in there."

"But what are they doing? And where are Joe and Steve?"

There was no sign of the other boys.

"Maybe they got cold feet."

"I think we should go," Tommy said. "I don't like this."

Garry held up a hand. "Listen!"

They listened. A low sound was coming from the church. It sounded like a chant.

"Oh, er!" Tommy said. "Come on. I'm going."

He began to turn his bicycle in readiness to ride away, but his companion stopped him. "Don't be a wet. There's nothing to be afraid of. I vote we go and take a look."

Tommy wavered uncertainly, but he reflected that if he went away he would have to ride back through the wood on his own, and it was too scary. So in the end he decided to follow the other boy's lead.

Garry was already leaning his bicycle against the wall of the churchyard, and Tommy followed suit.

"We'll go in by the west door," Garry said.

They had been in that way before. Nobody bothered to lock the doors of the old church nowadays, and when you went in by the west door you were in the tower. They had often climbed the steps to the top of the tower; you got a good view from up there, where you were above the tops of the trees. If their parents had known of these escapades they would have been in trouble. Not only was it trespassing on Major Parkin's property, but it was dangerous climbing an old tower that might be crumbling away. So they kept the secret and left their elders in blissful ignorance.

A rotting lychgate gave access to the churchyard in which the neglected headstones leaned in all directions like drunken revellers executing a macabre dance. Garry had a small pocket torch, and he led the way past the porch and round the tower to the west door. This door had in fact become wedged in a half-open position, and they were able to slip past it without difficulty.

The chanting sounded louder now that they were inside the church, but they did not pause where they were to listen to it. A stairway on the left led upward, and they climbed the steps and came out on to the minstrel gallery where long years ago musicians had accompanied the services. From this vantage point they were able to peer down into the main body of the church over a low wooden railing which partly screened them from view. It would have been difficult for anyone below to have seen them anyway, since the lighting, which was being provided by a number of gas lanterns, was concentrated in the eastward end, and especially in the chancel.

There were about twenty or thirty persons congregated in that part of the church, and they were of necessity all standing, the pews having long since been taken away to be used for other purposes. All were dressed in long black cloaks with cowls over their heads, like monks of the Black Friars order. They were facing the altar; for there was one; not draped in white, however, but in sombre black. And on it was no cross or candlestick, though behind was the head of a goat, horned and bearded and mounted on a pedestal.

The chanting continued, but it was difficult from the minstrel gallery to distinguish more than a few of the words. Once it sounded like: "We worship thee, Lord Lucifer." Then all bowed their heads and repeated several times on a rising note: "Lucifer, Lucifer, Lucifer!"

"What's Lucifer?" Tommy whispered.

"The Devil," Garry replied.

"Oh, er! I don't like it."

"Nor me neither."

"I wish I hadn't come."

"Me too."

But they both stayed there, awed but fascinated.

There was no carved screen between the nave and the chancel; it also had been removed, possibly for safekeeping, possibly to be used elsewhere. The cowled figures were standing some yards back from the altar steps, and now four others appeared from the Lady Chapel on the left of the altar. When the boys saw what these persons were carrying they drew breath sharply.

"Cor!"

It was a naked woman, long blonde hair trailing. They laid her on the black altar and drew back. The chanting continued. One of the four who had carried the woman in took a silver cup that was handed to him by one of the others, held it aloft in two hands and bowed three times to the goat's head. Then he poured some liquid, which looked like red wine, on to the woman's body. She appeared to shiver, but made no other movement and uttered no sound.

The man who had poured the wine, handed the cup back to the one he had taken it from and threw back his cowl. It was the first time any of them had bared their heads and the first opportunity the boys had had of getting a clear view of any of the faces. It came as a shock to them when they saw this one, because they recognised it immediately. The man was so well known in the district; indeed it was he who owned the land on which the church was built.

"Major Parkin!"

"Him!"

They would not have believed it if they had not seen it for themselves. A man like that, respected in the community, even looked up to as an example to others, taking part in such a blasphemous ceremony as this! It was really past belief, and yet it was happening.

And now something even more astounding was happening. The major was climbing on to the altar too; he was lying on top of the woman and doing something to her. He had drawn up the cloak so that the lower part of his body was bare, and they could see his legs moving.

"He's not," Tommy whispered. "He can't be."

"He bloody is."

"Cor!"

They knew they would never be able to tell this to anybody, not even to other boys. Because it would get out and they would be punished for telling lies, inventing scandal. Their fathers would lam them.

It was like a big black bat descended on the woman, pinning her down. They could see her head moving jerkily from side to side, the blonde hair all in a tangle. They could not tell whether she was making any sound because of the chant; she might have been moaning.

"Who is she?" Tommy asked.

"How should I know?"

"She looks pretty."

"Maybe not if she was closer, At that distance you can't tell."

Major Parkin got off the woman and adjusted his cloak; but she still lay there. The chanting had continued all the time, seeming to increase in volume, as though a kind of frenzy were taking hold of the assembled acolytes; as though they were aware that the ceremony was about to reach its climax.

"Now what happens?" Tommy whispered.

"I don't know."

"I think we ought to go now."

"I think so too."

"We should've gone sooner."

"Yes, we should."

But they did not move; they stayed where they were, crouched down, peering through the railing; shivering a little, not from the cold but because it was all so scary; something to give you bad dreams; something to make you wake sweating in the night.

"We'd had done better to stay in bed."

"I know, I know."

"Joe and Steve never came."

"Bet they never meant to."

And the worst was yet to come.

From somewhere under his cloak Major Parkin pulled out a dagger. He held it up to show the others; the light glinted on the steel blade. He bowed again to the goat's head; once, twice, three times.

"Hail, Lucifer! Hail, Lord!"

The dagger was poised above the woman and the chanting rose to a shout of ecstasy. Parkin appeared to brace himself for the final act and the dagger began to descend.

The woman seemed to realise at the last moment what was about to happen, to appreciate the danger she was in. She made a movement as if to avoid the blow, but was too late. The point of the dagger plunged into her. She screamed. Blood spurted.

The boys fled.

Chapter Thirteen – Something Different

JULIA had returned to London on the Monday. It was early on the Thursday when Hogan rang again. Rowan had had a quiet few days with no interruptions from the police or Josh Froggatt. Indeed, he had managed to get a little work done on his novel, and without further distractions he had begun to have some glimmering of hope for it.

Then the telephone rang.

Hogan said: "I've got another little surprise packet for you, Charlie."

Rowan groaned. "Not again! I thought you were giving it a miss."

Hogan laughed. "No rest for the wicked. Maybe that's a very appropriate saying, in the circumstances."

"So you admit you're wicked?"

"I was referring to you, Charlie. You aren't getting much rest, are you? How are you sleeping? Any nightmares?"

"The only nightmares I'm getting are when I'm awake."

"Is that so? Well, here's another one to go with the rest. Want to hear about it?"

"I'm going to, whether I want to or not, I suppose. So let's have it. Where've you left the body this time?"

Hogan chuckled. "This'll kill you, Charlie. In your garden."

Rowan was amazed; he could hardly believe it. What Hogan was telling him was that at some time during the night he had carried a dead body into the garden of the cottage and left it there. It must have been done when Rowan had been fast asleep, and he had not heard a sound. The audacity of the man was astounding; it was almost like leaving a corpse on the doorstep. And he had taken that risk; had no doubt driven up nearly to the gate. Suppose someone had seen him carrying the body in! But nobody had; that was certain. Nobody had seen a thing. It just showed what you could get away with if you had the nerve.

"There's another thing," Hogan said. "There's something special about this one. Something different."

"What's different about it?"

"You'll see when you find it."

"Hogan, you bastard!" Rowan shouted into the mouthpiece. "You filthy stinking bastard!"

But Hogan was not listening. He had rung off.

*

It was obviously not in the front garden; a body could not possibly have been hidden there. The garden at the back was a wilderness; he had neglected it and it was a mixture of weeds and coarse tufty grass and overgrown shrubs. The body could have been thrown down almost anywhere and it would have been obscured by the rampant growth. He searched but could not find it. After a long hot dry spell of weather the ground was hard and no footprints were visible. But then he noticed that there was a kind of track where the vegetation had been trampled down; and this track led to an old woodshed at the far end of the garden.

He went to the woodshed and pulled open the door. It was there, propped up against a pile of logs. Like the others, it was a woman; quite young, naked and with long fair hair. The eyes were open and staring, but they were seeing nothing; would never see anything again.

He saw at once what Hogan had meant when he had said that there was a difference about this one. It was in the method of killing: the other two had been strangled, but this woman had been stabbed, just once, probably through the heart. The wound was visible, and the dried blood. Rowan felt sick.

*

He had to go through it all again. But this time the circus descended on his own back garden; he could not get away from it.

"He's getting really cocky," Wint said. "Bringing it right up to your own doorstep. And he's changed the modus operandi too. That's curious; mostly they stick to the same method of killing. But your man is an original; he varies the pattern."

There was something else that distinguished this woman from the others: she had a small tattoo on her left arm above the elbow. It was in the shape of a rose.

Wint thought this might help in the identification. "Somebody must know about that, if only they'll come forward."

*

And on the Saturday someone did come forward. It was a London prostitute named Cynthia Anderson. She walked into a police-station early in the morning and said she had read in the paper about the body with the rose tattoo and she thought she knew who the victim was. She believed it might be a friend of hers named Jackie Byers, who had not been seen around for two or three days. She had seen the picture of the dead woman too, and thought it looked like Jackie.

She was asked why she had not revealed this the previous day when the report had appeared in the press, and she replied that she had needed time to think about it. She was not eager to go to the police; they were no friends of hers and it was only going to mean trouble for her. And besides, she might have been wrong about the picture, though the rose tattoo was a bit of a clincher. But she felt worried about Jackie and finally decided to tell the coppers what she knew.

She was taken down to Wingstead in a police car. The body was in the mortuary and it was shown to her. It was a shock, seeing that dead face; it made her feel quite faint. It also made her want to cry, because this had been such a lovely girl and she was too young to come to this. It wasn't right; not right at all.

"Well, do you recognise her?" Wint asked.

"Yes," she said. "That's Jackie."

They took her back to the police-station and took her to the interview room, and a woman police officer brought her a cup of tea and stayed while the detective chief inspector questioned her. He wanted to know when she had last seen Jackie, and she told him; she remembered it clearly enough.

"It was Tuesday evening. I was with her and this guy comes up in a car and calls to her."

"By name?"

"No, not by name. Just: 'Come here you with the blonde hair'. So I knew he didn't want me because, like you can see, I'm dark."

"What did he look like? Can you describe him?"

"Have a heart. The light was none too good and he was some way off. I never got a real close look at him."

"So you don't know whether he was young or old?"

"Not a clue really. All I can tell you is he had one of them upper-class voices. Not one of the usual riff-raff, if you know what I mean."

Wint saw that he was not going to get much help from this woman. It was frustrating, because she had actually seen the murderer, this mysterious Hogan; and apparently he had not been using the assumed accent at that time. But if she could tell him nothing about the man's personal appearance, what was the use of it?

"Can you remember what kind of car it was?"

"Well, I'm not good on cars; most of 'em look alike to me. But this was one of them high off the ground ones. Jackie had to climb up to get in it. You know, the go anywhere sort."

"A Range Rover?"

"Maybe."

"Colour?"

"Dark."

"Green?"

"Coulda been."

Wint sighed. There was all too much 'maybe' about it for his liking. It gave him nothing really solid to work on.

"When are you going to get him?" Miss Anderson demanded. "When are you going to catch the bugger?"

Wint would have been only too pleased if he could have given a confident answer to that question; but he could not. He said:

"Eventually."

She was not impressed. "This year, next year, sometime, never. You wanter get a move on. This is the third one he's killed, ain't it? That poor kid! What'd she done to deserve what she got?"

"She was in a dangerous profession."

"And I'm in it too. I could be the next one for the chop. Have you thought of that?"

"Yes, I have. And it may have been only the colour of your hair that saved you this time. My advice to you is to change your profession."

"Some hope!" she said. "Some bloody hope!"

*

Wint thought it right to tell Rowan that the latest victim had been identified. He told him who she was.

"So you were right about them being prostitutes and not local women."

"We can't be certain about the first one, but it seems likely she was too. And the second."

"Does it help?"

"Not a great deal. We still have no idea who the man is and haven't even got a description of him. All we know is that he speaks with an upper class accent."

Which ruled out Josh Froggatt, Rowan thought. But he had never really imagined that Froggatt was the man.

"What do you do now?"

"Keep hoping," Wint said.

Rowan had been planning to go up to Highgate for the weekend, but he had changed his programme after the discovery of the latest murder victim. He thought he had better hang around. Not that he could do anything to help.

He wondered whether Julia would propose coming down to the cottage instead, but apparently she had a commission that urgently needed to be completed, and would be busy. She was aghast at the news of the murder and seemed especially perturbed that the body should have been dumped on Rowan's own property.

"I wonder whether you should go on living there for the present."

"You really think I'm going to let that swine drive me out of my home?"

"Well —"

"Not a chance."

He thought about ringing her up again and telling her about the newest development, but decided not to. Meanwhile he could do nothing more productive than what the chief inspector was doing. He had to keep hoping.

*

On the Monday morning Wint's hopes received a boost. Two men and two boys walked into the police-station at Wingstead. The men looked grim and the boys looked uneasy.

One of the men said they wished to speak to someone in authority. He said his name was Drake and the other man's name was Mallet. The two boys were their sons, Tommy and Garry.

The constable manning the desk asked what they wanted to speak about, and Drake said it had to do with the murder inquiry. They had important information to give.

As luck would have it, Detective Chief Inspector Wint and Detective Sergeant Bilton had just come into the station, and in a very short time the men and the boys were in an interview room talking to these two officers.

The boys had kept silent about what they had seen in the old church until the Sunday after the event; but finally they had put their heads together and decided to make a clean breast of things to their fathers. By then there had been the third murder, and it was impossible for them to avoid the thought that there might be some connection between it and the ritual which they had witnessed. The secret was now too big for them to handle.

Mr Drake and Mr Mallet were both initially sceptical. They were next door neighbours in a pair of cottages in Little Madding, and the natural thing to do was for them to get together and discuss the matter. The boys were so adamant regarding what they had seen that it was impossible not to believe them. The question was, however, had they, in the uncertain light and at some distance, imagined more than they could actually be certain of? Suppose the ritual was some mummery indulged in by Major Parkin and his friends. There was no telling what the gentry might get up to; and if they carried a tale like this to the police they might end up making more than a little trouble for themselves.

They decided to sleep on it and see what it looked like in the morning. The next day, though still reluctant to become involved, they could not ignore the possible connection between the happenings in the old church and the stabbed body in Mr Rowan's woodshed. The similarity of the women, both blondes, and the method of killing was so remarkable that the matter could not be dismissed out of hand.

"We shall have to tell the police," Drake said. "It'll be for them to sort things out. We could get it in the neck if we do nothing. Withholding information, it's called."

Mallet had to agree. They wished their mischievous offspring had not let them in for this; but they had and there was no getting out of it.

Wint listened to the account, which he insisted on hearing from the boys themselves and not secondhand from their parents.

"Take your time," he said. "Let me have the story from start to finish. Don't leave anything out."

Thus prompted, they told the tale; Garry doing most of the talking and the younger boy chipping in now and then with a few details that had been missed out.

"So," Wint said when they had come to the end of the recital, "when you saw Major Parkin stab the woman and heard her scream you ran away? Is that so?"

"Yes," Garry said. "We were scared."

"But you saw the blood?"

"Oh, yes. It spurted. It was horrible."

"And you know nothing of what happened after that because you had run away?"

"Yes. We got on our bikes and rode as fast as we could."

"I can imagine you would," Wint said, and he gave a wintry smile. "That should be a lesson to you not to sneak out in the middle of the night to visit old churches."

"We won't do it again — ever," Garry said.

"I expect not. Though in this instance you may well have done us a service."

"You think it will help?" Mallet asked.

But the chief inspector was not committing himself on that point. "We shall see. But whatever happens I am obliged to you for coming forward. All of you."

Before they left he warned them to say nothing to anyone about the matter for the present. They promised to heed the warning.

*

When they had gone Wint had a talk with Bilton.

"What do you think of this story, Fred?"

"It's so crazy it has to be true. Those kids would never have made it up."

"Just what I think."

"Parkin, though. Seems such an unlikely murderer."

"Well, he's a devil-worshipper apparently; and anyone who's cranky enough to believe in that load of old junk would do anything, I'd guess."

"So you'd say he's Hogan?"

"I'm not sure I'd go as far as that yet. How about you?"

"Well, sir," Bilton said, "it all fits, doesn't it? The blonde woman, the method of killing, the Range Rover driven by the man who picked her up, the timing —"

"We don't know for certain he was driving a Range Rover. Miss Anderson only said it looked like that type of vehicle. And there's another thing: if Parkin is Hogan, why was only the last victim stabbed while the others were strangled?"

"Because this was the only one that was killed as part of the devil-worshipping ritual, perhaps?"

"Possible. But odd."

"The whole thing is odd," Bilton said.

Wint agreed. "That's true. Anyway, I think this is where we pay another visit to Astley Manor and have a little talk with our major."

Chapter Fourteen – No Murder

WINT and Bilton drove to Astley Manor armed with a search warrant. They found the house occupied only by Mrs Simmons and Maggie, the maid.

"Major Parkin is away," Mrs Simmons said. "He went away last Friday."

"Do you know where he went?" Wint asked.

"No, sir I don't. It may have been London. He often goes there. But he didn't tell me where he was going. He's like that; don't tell you much. Well, it's his business, that's what I say."

She took the two detectives into the kitchen when Wint said they would like a talk with her. It was more her ground than any of the other rooms, where she would have felt it presumptuous of her to entertain them.

"And did the major say when he would be coming back?" Wint asked.

"No, he didn't. He comes and goes as he pleases. I never know for certain when he'll be here."

"And that doesn't bother you?"

"Lor', no. Why should it? I just come in daily and get on with my work. If he's here I get his meals for him; if he isn't, I don't."

"And when he goes up to London does he ever bring anyone back with him?"

Mrs Simmons went on the defensive. "I don't think I should talk about anything like that. He mightn't like it. And it's not my business, is it?"

"But it is our business. And we are police officers making an investigation. So don't you think it would really be best if you answered our questions without any prevarication?"

"Well," she said, "if you put it like that —"

"I do put it like that. So now I'll ask you again — when Major Parkin makes these visits to London or anywhere else, does he ever bring anyone back with him?"

"There's the young women now and then, I must admit. But there's no harm in it, is there? If he wants a bit of female company, what I say is why not? It's not a crime, is it?"

Wint offered no judgement on this. He said: "How long do these women stay?"

"It varies. Sometimes a few days. Sometimes only the one."

"And then he takes them back?"

"I suppose so."

"Has there been one here lately? In the past week, say."

Mrs Simmons admitted that there had.

"When did she arrive?"

"It must have been some time last Tuesday evening."

"You saw her?"

"Not then, no. I'd gone home. But she was here the next morning. Maggie took her a cup of tea in bed."

"What was her name?"

"Jackie."

Chief Inspector Wint and Sergeant Bilton exchanged a meaningful glance. They seemed to be really getting somewhere now.

"Any surname?" Wint asked.

"Not as I heard of."

"Major Parkin didn't mention it?"

"No."

Wint took a photograph from his pocket and showed it to the housekeeper. "Is that her?"

Mrs Simmons put on a pair of glasses to examine the photograph and answered doubtfully: "I wouldn't like to say it is. And then again I wouldn't like to say it isn't."

"You can't be certain?"

"No, sir, I can't. These young blondes, they look so much alike with their hair down, don't they? And somehow they seem different in photos."

When Maggie was called in to give her opinion she was equally vague. In the presence of the police officers she seemed overawed and quite stupid. Wint felt like giving her a clout with his hand to knock some sense into her. But that would have been against the rules.

"Did anyone else see her?"

Mrs Simmons believed the gardener and his boy might have. "She went for a walk, you see."

Wint sent Bilton with the photograph to find these two people and obtain their opinion. When he returned he found the chief inspector drinking a cup of coffee that Mrs Simmons had made for him.

"Any joy?" Wint asked.

"Not much," Bilton said. "The gardener says it's her. The boy says it isn't."

Wint nodded. It was just about what might have been expected. Witnesses were notorious for their unreliability.

"Mrs Simmons tells me the woman left late on the Wednesday or very early the next day. She did not see her go. Jackie was still here when she went home but was gone before she came in in the morning. The bed had not been slept in."

"Ah!" Bilton said. Both he and the chief inspector were aware of the significance of this fact even if Mrs Simmons was not. He wondered whether she had guessed why they were asking these questions. She must have heard or read all about the latest murder and the discovery of the blonde in Rowan's garden; so she would have had to be very obtuse not to have suspected the connection. But if she had, she was not mentioning it.

"Did Major Parkin have any other visitors on the Wednesday evening?" Wint asked.

"He may have. There was a lot of dirty glasses I had to wash up in the morning, but I didn't see anyone. They must've come and gone after I left."

Wint finished his coffee and produced the search warrant, which he showed to Mrs Simmons. "This gives us authority to search the house. You understand?"

Mrs Simmons looked at the warrant, but he doubted whether she was reading it. She said:

"If you must, you must. It's your job, I suppose."

"Yes, it is our job."

*

They did not have to search far. In a kind of junk room on the second floor they found the goat's head, several black cloaks, a black cloth stained with what looked like dried blood and a dagger, also apparently with dried blood on the blade.

"Amazing," Wint said. "Didn't even bother to wash the murder weapon or hide any of the evidence." He spoke softly for Bilton alone to hear. Mrs Simmons had accompanied them in their search but she had not come into the junk room.

Bilton agreed. The working of the criminal mind was a mystery. It was as if the murderer were deliberately trying to give himself away. Or simply not caring one way or another.

The dagger, a poniard, was a collector's item. It was the kind of thing that an Elizabethan gentleman might have worn as the complement to his rapier. It had a chased hilt and a narrow pointed blade, and might have been of Italian origin.

Handling it carefully with a handkerchief, Bilton put it in a polythene bag; and when they went away he and Wint took it and the stained black cloth with them.

*

It was the next morning, the Tuesday, when Major Parkin, seated in the lounge of his usual hotel in Kensington, happened to read in the morning paper that he was a wanted man. According to the news item, the police investigating the third of what the journalists had now started calling 'The Telephone Murders' were searching for a Major Edward Millhouse Parkin, who they believed could assist them in their enquiries.

"Good God!" Parkin exclaimed. "It can't be. Surely they don't think I —
"

He was seriously perturbed. He was also greatly enraged. To have his name splashed across the front pages of the popular press in connection with a sordid murder case was disgusting. Something had to be done about it. And quickly.

He went immediately to the reception desk, demanded to have his bill made out, packed his bag, paid the account and checked out. He was not sure whether the receptionist had seen the item in the paper and noted the similarity of the names, but she said nothing.

Shortly after eleven o'clock he walked into the Wingstead police-station, announced that he was Major Parkin and expressed a desire to see the officer in charge of the murder investigation. Chief Superintendent Dwyer was not available and he had to be content with Chief Inspector Wint, who happened to be working in the incident room with Sergeant Bilton. Wint and Bilton were incredulous when told that the man they were looking for and believed to be on the run had voluntarily given himself up.

"You're sure it's him?"

"That's who he says he is, sir," the constable who had delivered the message said. "He seems very steamed up."

Wint discovered that this was a rather mild description of the major's state. He was hopping mad. He recognised Wint and Bilton at once from their earlier meeting.

"Now what the devil is going on? The damn papers say you've been looking for me."

"Well, yes, sir, we have," Wint admitted.

"What for, dammit, what for?"

"We think you may be able to help us."

"Yes, that's what I read in the paper. What do you mean by it, for God's sake?"

Wint suggested mildly that they should go somewhere a little less public and have a talk. He was beginning to have a few qualms. Parkin certainly did not act like a guilty man.

They went to the interview room with Parkin still fuming. Before starting the interrogation Wint gave the major the usual caution.

"Used in evidence!" Parkin exclaimed. "Evidence of what, may I ask?"

"It's the form," Wint said. "You may have your solicitor present if you wish, sir."

"Damn solicitors! Why should I want one? Any questions you care to ask I'll answer, but I warn you, you're barking up the wrong tree."

"That remains to be seen. Now sir, we have reason to believe that on the evening of the Tuesday of last week — August the twenty-first, that is — you picked up a prostitute in London and brought her down to your home, Astley Manor. Is that correct?"

Parkin hesitated and seemed to lose some of his self-assurance. Then he said in a more subdued tone of voice: "Yes, that is so. But it's not illegal, is it?"

"In itself, no. Whereabouts did you pick her up?

"Not far from Liverpool Street Station. That area."

"And what was the name of this woman?"

"Jackie."

"Did she give a surname?"

"No. They never do, do they?"

"Ah, so you've done this sort of thing before?"

"If you wish to know, yes."

"Oh, I do wish to know," Wint said. "I wish to know everything. So you brought this young woman to Astley Manor and she spent the night there. Right?"

"Dammit, yes."

"And the next day?"

"What about the next day?"

"What happened?"

"Nothing much."

"Oh, now really, Major, you can do better than that. I put it to you that quite a lot happened, especially in the evening and the night."

Parkin was startled; that was plain to see. Obviously he had not expected them to know so much. "What are you talking about?"

"I am talking about a gathering of kindred spirits at Astley Manor. I am talking about a kind of midnight ritual in the old ruined church on your estate. I am talking about the stabbing to death of the young woman named Jackie."

"No," Parkin burst out. "No, that's nonsense."

"You deny this happened?"

"Of course I deny it."

"Perhaps it would surprise you to learn that we have two witnesses to the whole affair."

"You can't have. None of them would have spoken of it. They are all sworn to secrecy. They have taken the oath."

"So now you admit that something did happen?"

"I admit nothing."

"But you see," Wint said, "the witnesses were not among those who were taking part. They were in the minstrel gallery unknown to you, and they saw it all. We have had a graphic description of the entire ceremony. And the witnesses recognised you."

"Who are these witnesses?" Parkin demanded.

"Never mind that for the present. Do you still maintain that the woman was not killed?"

"Certainly I do. Don't you see, Inspector, it was all symbolic. Like the Eucharist. The flesh and blood aren't real in that, are they? This was merely a symbolic sacrifice to the great Lord Lucifer."

"Devil-worship, you mean?" Bilton suddenly broke in.

"You may call it that."

"With the goat's head as the symbol of the Devil?"

"Precisely."

"We understand you had sex with the woman on the black altar," Wint said. "What was that the symbol of?"

"The rape of the virgin later to be sacrificed."

"With a symbolic virgin of course." Wint spoke ironically.

"Yes."

"And the stabbing. Was that also symbolic?"

"Certainly it was. Nothing more."

"The witnesses say she screamed and there was blood spurting."

"That's true. She was instructed in the part she had to play; but she was stupid. There was a polythene bag containing chicken's blood taped to the inside of her left arm. The dagger was to pierce this and release the blood. She would have come to no harm if she had not moved; but she did. The dagger pierced the bag but it also nicked her arm, and she bled a little. That is all."

"And afterwards?"

"We bandaged the arm and I took her back to London. She could have stayed on until the next morning but she was keen to get home, so I let her have her way."

Wint was not feeling so happy. Parkin was very glib, but was he telling the truth? One had to remember that as soon as the woman screamed the boys had fled. They had seen no more. He said:

"The woman who was found in the shed in Mr Rowan's garden has been identified. Her name was Jackie Byers. She had been stabbed. Probably on the very night when your ritual took place. She was a blonde too. The man who picked her up in London was driving a Range Rover. It fits, wouldn't you say?"

"I don't give a damn if it does fit." Parkin was red in the face. "It isn't the same woman. It can't be."

"And yet it seems all too likely from where I'm sitting," Wint said. "Of course you have a number of witnesses who might corroborate your story. If you would like to give us their names —"

Parkin gave a vehement shake of the head. "No. We are a brotherhood sworn to secrecy, as I said. I refuse to name them."

Wint shrugged. "I can't force you to. And anyway, they would hardly be reliable witnesses. They would be bound to back you up. After all, being accessory to murder is a serious crime."

"There was no murder. Damn you, there was no murder."

Chapter Fifteen – No Answer

ROWAN rang up Julia at her Highgate house. "I suppose you heard that the police have been looking for Major Parkin?"

"Oh, yes. I read it in the paper. It seems they think he can help with their inquiries. Does that mean they suspect him of being the murderer?"

"I don't know. But I've just heard that he gave himself up at Wingstead police-station and that he's still there, so it begins to look as if they've got something on him."

"But surely it couldn't be him. Could it?"

"I don't know that either. All I know is that I haven't heard a thing from Hogan since he told me where to find the last body, and it isn't like him to be silent for so long. So if Parkin is Hogan —"

"Oh God, I do hope they've got the right man. It would be a tremendous relief. Do you really think it could be?"

"I'm sure it could be. All the opportunity was his, wasn't it? A local man, knowing the place, even owning part of it. Who would have been better able to do it all?"

"But why? I mean why pick on you?"

"Perhaps he took a dislike to me when we were introduced at that Tory do."

"Well, I hope it's finished now. I do hope it is."

"So do I," Rowan said. "For both our sakes."

*

Unfortunately, it was not finished. A report from the forensic scientist came through, which blew Wint's case against Major Parkin clean out of the water. The blood on the dagger was indeed as the major had maintained mainly chicken's, as was that on the black cloth. There were also traces of human blood on the dagger, but this too only bore out Parkin's story. Moreover, it was quite impossible for the dagger to have been used to kill the woman with the rose tattoo, since the nature of the wound indicated that it had been inflicted by something more like a broad-bladed knife than a thin stiletto.

The clincher was the discovery by the Metropolitan Police in the region of Liverpool Street Station of a prostitute with a bandaged left arm who went by the name of Jackie Jones. She did not need a great deal of urging to admit that she had indeed been picked up by a man she knew only as the major, and had been taken to his place in the country. There she had taken part in some kind of play-acting in an old church.

"It was crazy. All these idiots dressed up in long black cloaks and this goat's head they was bowing to, and me naked on a kind of table covered with a black cloth. I was supposed to be a sacrifice to somebody called Lucifer, and I had this bag of hen's blood strapped to my arm, which the major was supposed to stab so's the blood ran out and it looked like he was stabbing me. It'd have been all right if he hadn't made a balls-up of it and cut my arm. I was supposed to scream, but I didn't have to do no acting when that happened; it bloody hurt. But he was good about it, I must say. Paid me a bit extra as compensation and then brought me home, driving through the night. I went to sleep in the car, but it was all that crazy, you wouldn't believe."

But they did believe. And Wint had to believe too, and had to let Major Parkin go. Parkin went breathing fire and threatening to sue the police for wrongful arrest, but Wint was pretty sure he would never do that; he had had enough unwanted publicity as it was, and it would all take some living down.

*

Hogan broke his silence and came on the line to gloat.

"Well, well, well, Charlie boy! So they nabbed the wrong man. Too bad. Fancy thinking it was old Major Parkin. He's a nut-case sure enough, but I doubt whether he ever killed anybody even when he was in the army. I know him. Oh, I know all about him too; and all his funny little ways."

"You're a friend of his?" Rowan asked.

"Friend! Oh, that's a joke. Me a friend of his. That really is a joke, that is. Almost as good as the idea of my being a friend of yours."

So he was not pretending any more. It had gradually come to this: the point where he was quite openly an enemy and making no secret of the fact. As Wint had predicted, it had all been leading up to this.

"It's going to get worse, you know, Charlie boy. Soon now. This is the run-in. We're getting to it. The climax. There has to be a climax in all the best stories, doesn't there? You know that. It's what everything that's gone

117

before leads up to in the end. And it's coming closer, closer. Remember that, Charlie, remember it. And sleep well."

He rang off.

*

Rowan put another call through to Julia. It seemed an age since he had seen her. All this Hogan business was not only dealing a blow to his writing, it was also mucking up his love life. And maybe that was all part of Hogan's plan.

He told her that the man had surfaced again.

"Oh, God!" she said. "What was it this time? Not another body?"

"No. This was more of an ego trip for him. He wanted to crow over the fact that the police had picked up the wrong man and then had to let him go."

She had heard about that of course, and she was not feeling happy. "I wish you were here, Charles. I miss you. Why don't you come over right now?"

It was the Friday afternoon, and he thought about it. But there were a few things he needed to attend to. He suggested coming the next morning.

"I could stay for a few days, possibly the whole of next week. How does that strike you?"

"It would be lovely. You can tear yourself away from your book?"

"Are you kidding? The book seems to have got away from me. I think I may have to scrap it."

"Oh, no. Not after all the work you've put into it. That would be just too terrible."

"It happens sometimes. The house of cards collapses. Anyway, I'll be seeing you tomorrow."

"I'll look forward to it. I love you, Charles."

"And I love you, Julia."

*

It was Detective Sergeant Bilton who came to pick up the tape of Hogan's latest call.

"I don't think you'll find anything on it to give you a lead," Rowan told him. "It's all much as before. Except that he's hinting that things are coming up to a climax."

"He said that?"

"Yes. He seems to be threatening me openly now. There's no mask of good fellowship left; that's all done away with. He'd heard about you

118

having to let Parkin go, and he was laughing about that. Incidentally, he also gave the impression that he's quite well acquainted with the major and doesn't much like him."

"That's interesting," Bilton said. "It's another pointer to a local man."

"That's what I thought. Somebody with a grudge against Parkin as well as against me?"

"Perhaps. But I'd still say you're the prime target and I don't like this suggestion that things are approaching a climax. You're at risk, Mr Rowan; can't be any doubt about that."

"So do I get police protection now?"

"I'm afraid not. It's out of the question. You'll just have to be on your guard. Lock up well at night."

"You think that would keep him out? There are still windows."

Bilton shrugged. "Nowhere is absolutely safe from intruders. You'd need a concrete house with no windows or doors."

"Which would be rather inconvenient. Perhaps I should buy a gun."

"You would need a permit. And I don't think you'd get one."

"Well, I'm going up to London tomorrow and I shall be staying there for a few days."

"With Miss Spence?"

"Yes. Should be safe enough there. Hogan won't know where she lives."

But the sergeant was not so sure about this. "Her name has been in the news; she's a painter and I suppose not unknown in the art world. He's smart enough to have found that address in Highgate; you can be pretty certain of that."

Rowan had to agree with Bilton's reasoning, and it did nothing to make him feel any happier. Because if Hogan knew Julia's address, might he not strike at her first? Might that not be what he had been hinting at when he had said that things would get worse? Suppose the next time he rang through it were to be with directions leading to another dead body. And suppose when that body was found it turned out to be Julia's.

But no. Hogan just went for blonde prostitutes, didn't he? And Julia was a brunette and was certainly not a prostitute. So did that make her safe? Of course it did not. Hogan was not one of those serial killers who never altered their methods; already he had switched from strangulation to stabbing; and because of some strange twist in his mind the entire purpose of the operation seemed to be to strike at him, Charles Rowan. It had all been building up to that, and what more vital blow could be struck than the killing of the woman he loved?

Bilton was saying: "We thought we had him in the bag and it came to nothing. Now we seem to be back to square one. I suppose we shall just have to keep on trying."

When he had left Rowan did some heavy thinking, and his thoughts were gloomy. He wondered whether to change his plans and go up to Highgate that evening. But surely nothing would happen as soon as that. Though, on the other hand, why should it not? There was no telling when Hogan might act; he was not one to give a date beforehand.

He wavered for the rest of the afternoon and early evening, unable to make up his mind and even unable to get down to the tasks he had proposed doing. Finally, as it was growing dusk he came to a decision: he would ring Julia and tell her that he would after all be travelling up to London that evening and that she could expect him within the next couple of hours or so.

He dialled the number and heard the ringing note; but no one picked up the instrument at the other end of the line. He kept it going for quite a while before giving up. And now he was even more worried. He told himself that there was no reason to be; that Julia had simply gone out for some reason or other; that she was maybe visiting a neighbour; that she had gone to a nearby public-house to stock up for the projected visit; anything —

None of the things he told himself had the slightest effect in relieving his anxiety; he just went on worrying. He decided to give it another hour and ring again.

He did so. There was no answer.

That settled it. He would leave it no longer. He would get the car out and drive up to London without further delay. He ought to have gone that afternoon. He ought to have done as she suggested. She had asked him to go and he had put it off. And now God knew what had happened to her.

He had packed a bag and was just leaving the cottage when the telephone rang. He had half a mind to ignore it, but there seemed to be an imperious quality to the sound and it could not be ignored. He went back into the study and lifted the receiver.

"Hello, Charlie boy," Hogan said. "This is your old friend speaking. I have a message for you."

Chapter Sixteen – Into the Open

SHE was about to close the French windows when she glimpsed a movement in the dusk of the garden. The thought leaped immediately into her mind; someone is there, by the shrubs; an intruder.

She called out: "Who is that? What are you doing?"

There was no answer, but the figure moved closer and became more visible. It advanced into the light spilling out from the sitting-room. She saw that it was a man, but still the face was too shadowy for her to see it clearly.

"Don't you know who I am?" the man said. "Haven't you been expecting me? I know you, Julia. And I know Charlie. He and I have become quite familiar to one another on the telephone."

He came closer and she saw that he had a gun in his right hand, a flat black automatic pistol, not very large but undoubtedly lethal.

"Oh, my God!" she said. "You're Hogan, aren't you?"

"So you've guessed at last," he said. "Well, good for you."

"What are you doing here? What do you want? How did you get in?"

"As to getting in," he said, "it was perfectly easy. I simply walked in."

She could see that, as he had said, it had been easy for him. There was a brick archway at the side of the house, giving access to the garden at the back. There was a door in the archway, but it was never locked. He had opened it and walked in. He must have done it very quietly, for she had heard nothing.

"And as to what I am doing here. Why, Julia, I should have thought you could have guessed. I have come for you."

"No!" she breathed; and the thought of those dead women came into her head, uninvited and unwelcome. She looked at the gun in his hand. It was not pointing at her. Not yet. But it frightened her nonetheless. There was potential death for her also in that piece of dull black metal. "No!"

"Yes," he said, mocking her. "Yes."

And then he said: "Go back into the room."

She retreated from the French windows backwards, and he followed close behind her. She could see him clearly now, and saw that he had grown one of those so-called designer beards that made men look like ruffians even when they were not. He was wearing jeans and a leather jacket with a zip-fastener, and soft black leather shoes with polyurethane soles. These things she noted automatically.

"Are you going to kill me?" she asked. She was trying to keep her voice from trembling, but it shook a little nevertheless. It was impossible to contemplate a violent death without a sense of fear, of terror even. She thought again of the two women strangled by this man, of the other woman stabbed to the heart. Was she to be the first of his victims to be shot with a pistol? Was that to be her distinction?

He seemed amused by her question. "Are you afraid, my sweet Julia?"

She was angered by his use of the possessive and the endearment before her name. He had no right. But she answered simply: "Of course I am afraid. Who wouldn't be?"

"Indeed, who wouldn't?" He put the gun in a pocket of the leather jacket. "But your death is not imminent. It may become necessary later, but we shall see. We are going on a journey, you and I. And at the end of the journey, quien sabe, as the Spanish say. Who knows?"

"I will go nowhere with you," she said.

He shook his head, a smile of mockery on his lips. "Julia, Julia, you have no choice. You must and you shall come with me."

She saw him take a small bottle of liquid and a pad of lint from his pocket. And at that moment the telephone rang. It startled her. Her nerves were on edge and the sudden noise made her jump. Then she moved towards the instrument.

"Leave it," Hogan said.

She hesitated, undecided whether to obey or whether to grab the telephone and give a cry for help before he could prevent her. She guessed that it might be Charles calling, and she needed him; she really needed him as never before. She almost did it; it was touch-and-go for a moment; but in the end she lacked the nerve. She gave a sigh and her shoulders drooped in submission.

"Wise girl," Hogan said. "It would have done you no good."

They waited for the ringing to stop. It went on for quite a while but eventually ceased.

Hogan still had the bottle and pad in his hands. Now he took the cork from the bottle and wetted the pad with the liquid. It gave off a sickly sweet odour. He re-corked the bottle and put it back in his pocket. He did all this deliberately and without haste, while she watched as if mesmerised. She knew what was happening, what was about to happen, but she felt unable to make any move to avoid it.

"Now," Hogan said, "I must ask for your co-operation. If you do not give it I have to use force. Are you going to be sensible?"

Suddenly the spell was broken; she came to life. She shouted vehemently: "No, no, no!" And she turned and made a dash for the door of the room. She reached the door, but before she could open it he was on to her like a wolf. His left arm went round her neck, holding her, while his right hand pressed the pad over her mouth and nose. She struggled briefly, but he was too strong for her; and then the chloroform began to take effect and she sank into oblivion.

*

When she regained consciousness she was completely disorientated. She could not tell where she was. She was lying on a very hard surface like concrete, and above her she could see the night sky. The moon was shining and the stars were dimmed by its light. There appeared to be low walls all round her in a square which was only a few feet across. At the corners there appeared to be small pinnacles, and those on one side were casting shadows.

When she tried to move she discovered that her wrists were tied together in front of her and that her ankles were also tied. However, after something of a struggle she succeeded in sitting up, and she could see now that the low walls were in fact a battlemented parapet surrounding the square within. And then it came to her suddenly, though she could hardly believe it possible, that she was at the top of a church tower.

So the man who chose to call himself Hogan must have carried her up there. She was amazed at the feat of strength that must have entailed, even though she was of slender build. And why had he brought her there? For what purpose? Where, too, was this church? She could hear no sound; she seemed to be completely isolated. Had he abandoned her? That seemed hardly likely. But where had he gone?

Her head ached and she was feeling sick, but she managed to get herself into a position in which she could sit with her back supported by the parapet. She was more comfortable in her body like that, but there was no comfort in her mind. She knew that Hogan would return; and what would he do then? He was mad, utterly mad; she was convinced of that now; and a madman was capable of doing anything, unhindered by any thoughts of morality or law.

The night air was cool and she shivered. She was wearing cotton slacks and a crew-neck sweater over a blouse, but these were not enough to keep her warm and she was unable to take any exercise by moving around.

My God, she thought, what a plight I'm in! What can I do? What on earth can I do?

And the answer to that, of course, was simple. She could do precisely nothing.

*

Hogan sounded in pretty good spirits, Rowan thought. And he took that as a bad sign.

"What message?" he asked. "Let's have it."

"I've got Julia."

It took a moment or two for this to sink in. Then it was like a blow to the heart.

"You've got her?"

"Yes. Surprises you, doesn't it? Shocks you too, I shouldn't wonder."

"Damn you, Hogan! Where is she?"

"In a safe place. Couldn't be safer. And unharmed — as yet."

It was the last two words that contained the threat and touched him on the raw. He shouted into the telephone: "You swine, Hogan! If you dare to do anything to her I'll kill you. I swear it."

"You'll do nothing, Charlie." Hogan was contemptuous. "Can't you get it into your thick head that I'm the one that holds the winning hand? I give the orders and you carry them out if you want to save your lady love. You carry them out to the letter. Do you understand?"

Rowan swallowed his anger; because Hogan was right; he was in the driving seat and that fact had to be accepted.

"All right. Tell me what I have to do."

"First of all I'll tell you what not to do. Don't call the police. Do that and Julia is dead meat. And I don't have to convince you that when I say that I mean it. You've seen what I can do."

"Yes, I've seen."

"So no police. Right?"

"Right."

"Next order then. Get your car out and drive along the Little Madding road as far as the black barn. Do you know where that is?"

Rowan did. It was an old building, scarcely ever used now, some half a mile or so from Flint Cottage.

"I know."

"Good. When you get to the barn take your car off the road on to the cart track at the side of the building, switch the lights off and wait. Got that?"

"I've got it."

"Okay then. And remember what I said. No police."

He rang off.

*

Rowan knew that the proper thing to do would be to ignore Hogan's warning and alert the police at once. Hogan was obviously planning to make contact with him at the black barn, and if the police were there in hiding they could catch him without difficulty. But there were two snags to this scenario. Number one: it would take time to get the police there, and Hogan would be expecting him to arrive in just a few minutes. If there was any appreciable delay he would become suspicious and make tracks before the forces of the law turned up. And number two: if by any chance they did succeed in catching him he might refuse to tell where Julia was hidden; and a cunning bastard like him might have put her in some place that would take so long to find that she would be dead before they got to her.

He dared not take the risk. He had to play the game Hogan's way and hope for the best.

*

There was hardly any traffic on the road to Little Madding, and in a few minutes he was at the black barn. The farm track at the side had once had a gate, but this had long since vanished and it was now open to the road. Rowan backed his car on to the track and stopped it about ten yards from the road. He switched off the engine and the lights, released the seat-belt and waited.

Hogan appeared suddenly from behind the barn and tapped on the window of the car. Rowan opened the door and looked at Hogan and knew who he was. He had seen the man just once before and there was only the moonlight to reveal his face; but he knew.

"You!"

"So you remember me," the man said. And he was not using the coarse accent of the character known as Hogan but the more polished voice of Peter Dacre. The deception was finished and he had come out into the open.

125

"I remember you," Rowan said. "I should have guessed."

Yet how could he have done so? Nothing had pointed to Dacre. And had he not been out of the country when the first killing had taken place? In Brazil. But that was only what he had told Julia, and of course he had been lying. This was obvious now, but it had not been so at the time. Julia had not thought of asking him for proof that he had been in Brazil; it would not even have occurred to her to doubt his statement.

"No, you shouldn't," Dacre said. "You had no reason to suspect me. Though somehow I think you realised I was your enemy that time when Julia introduced you to me,"

"Yes, I did. But not every enemy goes to such lengths to vent his spite as you've done."

"No, I'm rather special," Dacre said. "But at least I read your books, so I did you some good." He gave a laugh. "I thought they might give me an insight into what made you tick."

"And did they?"

"Oh, yes. A novelist gives a lot of himself away in his books. Unwittingly perhaps. And then of course I had this marvellous idea of getting at you that way. It was quite brilliant, don't you think?"

Rowan was amazed at the conceit of the man. He was so proud of what he had done. But the very fact that he was revealing all this looked bad. It showed that he was not afraid of Rowan's giving him away to the police because he knew that Rowan would never be in any position to do so. Dead men told no tales.

And of course he craved an audience. Where would be the satisfaction in being so clever if there was no one to reveal your cleverness to? Rowan was not only his enemy and his victim; he was his confidant too.

"Get out of the car," Dacre said. And Rowan saw now that he had a pistol in his hand. "We have to walk a little way from here."

Rowan did as he was told. He locked the car and put the keys in his pocket, It seemed to amuse Dacre.

"You don't want anyone to steal it while you're away?"

"There's a lot of car thieving about," Rowan said. "And incidentally, you don't need the gun. I'm coming with you willingly, you know."

"That's true." Dacre stowed the pistol away in his pocket. "This way."

He began walking and Rowan followed. He kept to the road for a short distance, heading in the direction of Little Madding; but then he turned off on to a track that led into a wood. It was darker under the trees where the moonlight came through only in patches, but Dacre seemed to have no difficulty in finding his way.

"What I don't understand," Rowan said, "is how you come to know this neighbourhood so well. It's as if you'd lived here."

"I have. As a boy. I was brought up here. Does that surprise you?"

"It does rather. I would never have taken you for a country boy."

"My father was estate agent for Major Parkin's father, and I had the run of the place."

"Ah, that explains a lot."

"Does, doesn't it? But my father gave up that job when I was still a boy. Decided he could make more money working for himself. He was right; he had the Midas touch. Made a fortune in the City. Then died of a heart attack from the stress. My mother was already dead and I copped the lot, more or less."

"Nice for you."

"Wasn't it? You can do such a lot with money. It opens the whole bloody world to you. Here's my car. We ride the rest of the way."

It was standing at the side of the track, hardly visible under the trees; but a close look revealed to Rowan that it was a Jeep Cherokee.

"So it wasn't a Range Rover after all."

Dacre laughed. "Surprise, surprise! They got that wrong. It was old Zak Smith in the first place. Now what would he know about cars? But he set them all off on a false trail, suspecting everybody in the district who owned a Range Rover. What a joke! Get in."

They both got in, and Dacre started the Cherokee and they moved off along the woodland road, headlamps probing the way ahead.

"Where are we going?" Rowan asked.

"To church, actually," Dacre said. "Do you happen to be religious?"

Rowan got it then. "You mean the old church where Major Parkin —"

"Where Major Parkin had his little party? None other. That was another good joke."

Rowan supposed Dacre must have read about the devil-worshipping ritual in the morning papers. Somehow the press had got hold of the story from Drake and Mallet, who would have seen no reason to keep silent about it after the release of Major Parkin. And no doubt it had been made worth their while to talk.

"It was a bonus for me too," Dacre said. "Something I didn't even plan. Hiding the first two bodies on his property was a way of getting at him. I knew it would embarrass the pompous little sod."

"But why would you want to get at him?"

"Oh, I hate the bastard. He was always giving me hell when I was a kid and home for the holidays. He was a lot older than me, and as the young squire he could get away with the bullying, of course. Oh, he was a top-class bully, I can tell you. Caught me once taking pheasant's eggs from a nest and beat me with a stick. Maybe he's forgotten all that, but I haven't."

Rowan wondered how old Dacre was. At first he had taken him to be in his early thirties, but now he would have guessed that he was closer to forty. Maybe ten or a dozen years younger than Parkin.

"And now," Dacre said, "all this other stuff has come out. I certainly couldn't have planned that. His name will be mud in county society. He'll be ostracised. And you can bet your life the local Tories won't want to have anything to do with a Satanist. Not that your life is much of a bet right now. Well, here we are. This is where things begin to get really interesting."

Chapter Seventeen – Ill Met by Moonlight

THE old church was starkly revealed in the moonlight. Rowan had never seen it before, although he had lived within easy distance of it for quite a while. Now he thought it looked oddly menacing, though this could have been simply because of the manner in which he had been brought to it, and the possible consequence of that bringing.

Dacre parked the Cherokee outside the graveyard and led Rowan through the lychgate and round to the west door, which was still open. He took a small torch from his pocket, and with a word to Rowan to follow close behind, began the climb to the top of the tower. When Rowan stepped out into the open he did not immediately notice Julia sitting with her back to the parapet; but she saw him and gave a cry.

"Charles!"

He saw her then, and went quickly to her, noting the bound wrists and ankles, angered that Dacre should have done this to her. He bent down and started tugging at the knotted cord, intent on freeing her. But Dacre said sharply:

"Leave her!"

He turned and saw that the gun was again in Dacre's hand and that it was pointing at him.

"So this is where you brought her. This is where you would have left her to die if the police had caught you."

"Is that what you think?"

"What else would you expect me to think?"

"Frankly," Dacre said, "I expect nothing from you except to obey my orders. You must admit that you are at my mercy. I have been playing a game with you, Charlie, as you well know; a cat-and-mouse game with you as the mouse. You never had a chance of course; I was always going to win in the end. But I enjoyed spinning things out; it amused me."

"And all because of the green-eyed monster — jealousy. All this enmity because a woman threw you out and chose me instead. Is that what drove you out of your mind? Or were you always as crazy as a coot?"

"I am not crazy." There was an edge to Dacre's voice which Rowan noted with satisfaction. He was getting through the man's guard as he had done once before on the telephone when Dacre had been speaking in the guise of Hogan. Apparently he could not bear the suggestion that there was madness in him. "You had better not say that."

"Why not? Can't you take the truth? Who but a madman would go round killing whores and ringing up a man he hated to tell him where to find the bodies? Does that strike you as the action of a sane person?"

"It was genius, not insanity."

"Oh, I see. You are one of these lunatics who think they are Einstein, or maybe Napoleon or Genghis Khan."

"I am not a lunatic." Dacre's voice had risen. He was waving the pistol about. "You had better take care what you say, or else —"

"Or else you will shoot me? But isn't that what you intend to do anyway? Isn't that why you've brought me here?"

Dacre controlled himself with an effort. "Don't imagine I can't see what you are trying to do. You think you can goad me into doing something rash, so that you can perhaps rush at me and catch me off balance. It will not work. Even if you grappled with me you would be the loser. I am stronger than you in all ways, including the physical. I have been exercising my body while you have been sitting at your desk writing your stupid novels. Why, I could break your back if I wished."

Here he is boasting again, Rowan thought; this time about his physical strength. Yet the man must have a weakness if one could only find it and work upon it. So was that weakness his vanity, his overweening conceit? Perhaps. But how to use it against him; that was the problem.

And then Julia chipped in. "Be sensible, Peter. Do no more killing. What will you gain by it?"

"Satisfaction," Dacre said.

"No, Peter; you can't believe that. You must have some better feelings in you. You can't be all bad."

He sneered. "That's not what you said when you threw me over. You didn't see any good in me then, as I recall. You told me so. So why am I expected to be any better now?"

"In the heat of the moment we all say things we don't really mean."

"It's in the heat of the moment that the truth comes out. Anyway, that is neither here nor there. Now suppose I make you an offer. I spare Charlie boy's life and you come back to me. How does that strike you?"

Rowan knew that it was not a genuine offer. It would never work. Here was a man wanted for murder, and how could he be sure they would not give him away even if he extracted a promise from them not to do so? He himself must be fully aware of that, and he was still playing his little game, revelling in the godlike power he had over them.

Julia made no reply to the offer, but Rowan said: "We know you're only fooling. You like killing; it's part of the madness in you; it makes you feel good, doesn't it? Killing those women: I'd say you got a real kick out of that."

"What would you know about it? You would never have the courage."

"So it takes courage, does it? So why always women? Why never a man? Not quite enough courage for that?"

"You're a man," Dacre said. He raised the pistol and aimed it at Rowan.

Julia screamed: "No! Please, Peter! I'll do anything you want, anything."

Dacre gave a laugh and lowered the gun. "Now you're talking. You would really come back to me to save his life?"

"Yes."

"Well now, that's interesting. But I'm not sure; I'm really not sure. You see, I'd always be thinking you'd done this just for him; that it was him you loved and you were making this sacrifice only for his sake, not because of any feeling you had for me. It would rather tend to sour things between us, wouldn't it? I mean the relationship would hardly be a happy one; not happy at all. No; on second thoughts I'm afraid I shall have to withdraw the offer. Perhaps the plain fact is that I've lost the desire for you. I'm sure you will find that hard to believe, but really you no longer have any great attraction for me. I'm sorry if that offends you, but one must face facts. I wouldn't have you back now as a gift. Not after him."

He uttered the final words with a sudden burst of venom, spitting them out as a snake might spit its poison.

It silenced her. She seemed to realise that it was useless to plead with him. He was too eaten up with hate. It was that which had driven him from the outset and was driving him still.

Rowan knew this. He knew that it was Dacre's intention to kill them both, and that he was merely delaying the execution in order to satisfy a sadistic desire to tantalise them, to toy with them before, godlike, he cast them into oblivion. He had the gun and in the end would use it.

If he was not stopped.

Dacre said: "I have an alternative offer. It will be a test of your love, Charlie, for dear Julia. Do you think you could make a sacrifice for her? What I believe has been called the supreme sacrifice."

"Now what have you got in your nasty little mind?" Rowan asked.

"Just this. If you jump from this tower I will spare Julia's life. Now how does that sound to you?"

"It sounds to me like a way of saving you the bother of using the gun. I kill myself instead of you killing me."

"Oh, I don't know. Perhaps you would survive the fall."

"From this height! Do you really believe that possible?"

"By a miracle perhaps. Where better for a miracle to take place than this? Anyway, it would be an interesting experiment."

"I fancy I would very soon lose interest in it," Rowan said. He moved to the parapet and looked down. In the moonlight the ground seemed far below. Forty feet? Fifty perhaps? A fall from that height had to be fatal.

And of course Dacre would kill Julia anyway; the sacrifice would be quite in vain; it would be just another piece of amusement for that bastard. But he had no intention of providing him with that entertainment; he would not make the jump. It would be better to die by the bullet than that.

He said: "Come and take a look. It's a long way down."

"Oh, Charlie, Charlie!" Dacre said. "Do you have to be quite so transparent? You wish me to come close enough for you to take me off guard and push me over. Isn't that it?"

It was indeed what Rowan had had in mind, but he had never really believed it would work. Dacre was far too crafty to fall into that trap.

"Well, it was worth a try."

He moved back from the parapet, keeping his distance from Dacre, who still had the pistol in his hand and was watchful.

"I think you should take a look all the same, just to give you some idea of what you're asking me to do. I'll stay over here, so you'll be quite safe. Go on, Peter; you're not afraid of heights, are you? Or do you suffer from vertigo when you look down from a high place? Is that your trouble?"

"Don't be stupid," Dacre said. "I climbed up here, didn't I? I carried Julia up. I doubt whether you could have done that."

"Yes, but did you look down?"

"That's neither here nor there."

"So you are afraid to look down. You simply dare not go to the parapet and peep over the edge."

"Of course I'm not afraid." Dacre spoke angrily. Under Rowan's taunting he was beginning to lose his temper.

"Are you so sure? I can quite understand it if you are afraid. There are a lot of people like that and you could be one of them. It's nothing to be ashamed of. It's called a fear of heights."

"I know what it's called. And I have never suffered from it in my life."

"I would find that easier to believe if you gave a demonstration," Rowan said. "To me it seems that you are simply terrified of doing so."

He had touched the nerve at last, the weakness that he had been probing for, the vanity that would not permit Dacre to ignore this accusation of cowardice.

"Damn you! I will show you."

He walked to the parapet and looked down. And in that instant Rowan went for him in a wild rush that took him across the intervening space in moments.

But it was not done quite quickly enough. Dacre heard him coming and fired the pistol on the turn, not pausing to take aim. The bullet caught Rowan in the left arm just above the elbow; and it was like a hammer striking him. Yet such was the impetus of his forward lunge that it still carried him forward and his right shoulder hit Dacre in the chest. He gave a cry and tumbled over the parapet and vanished from sight.

Rowan was on his knees, the bone in his left arm shattered, blood flowing from the wound. He felt sick and in pain and yet glad. Because the thing had worked: Dacre's conceit had compelled him to take the bait even though he knew it for what it was. For a moment he had dropped his guard, and now he was gone and the threat was lifted. So there was reason to be glad.

But then suddenly he heard Dacre's voice, hoarse and pleading. "Help me!"

He could not believe it. Dacre was dead; he had to be. You could not fall from that height to the hard ground and still be alive. Yet the voice came again; he had not imagined it, and it seemed to emanate from a place quite close by. Which also was impossible.

Nevertheless, he managed to pull himself up with the aid of his good right arm and peer over the parapet. And there sure enough was Dacre, still alive and calling desperately for help. By some chance in a million he had in falling succeeded in clutching one of the gargoyles that projected from the sides of the tower; and now he was hanging by his arms, his legs dangling over a sheer drop to the pathway below.

He saw Rowan and pleaded again. "Help me!"

Rowan knew that it was out of the question. How could he, with only one usable arm, possibly lift the man back to safety? With two good arms it might have been done, though only with difficulty and at some risk to himself; but with just one it would have been the feat of a Samson.

And yet he tried it. He leaned over the parapet and reached down. His right hand almost touched the gargoyle, and Dacre made a grab at it and got half a grip. Rowan felt the sudden tug, and for a moment it seemed that he too would be dragged over the parapet and both of them would plunge to the ground as one. But Dacre's fingers could not retain their hold; they slipped from Rowan's hand and his grasp on the gargoyle gave way also. He uttered a long despairing cry and plummeted to the ground.

Chapter Eighteen – Only Fiction

JULIA came to visit him daily in the hospital. For the present she was living in Flint Cottage, which was convenient for getting to Wingstead. He feared that she was neglecting her painting, but she said she could make up for it later on when he was up and about again. He was getting on pretty well, but Dacre's bullet had done a lot of damage to his arm and it would be a while before he was able to use it properly again.

After Dacre had fallen to his death they had still had something of a problem getting away from the church tower, because Julia had been able to do nothing with her wrists and ankles securely bound; while he had been in considerable pain and bleeding freely.

Nevertheless, he had managed to unravel the knot on her wrist bond with his one good hand, and with her own free she had been able to untie her ankles. The descent had not been too difficult, although he was feeling somewhat giddy and almost fell once or twice. Outside the tower they had been obliged to pass the mangled body of Peter Dacre, looking grotesque in the moonlight. But they had ignored it and had taken the Cherokee, which still had the ignition key in it. Julia had driven straight to the hospital at Wingstead, and he had nearly passed out on the way. But after that there had been no more to do except leave it to the professionals to get on with the job.

Those other professionals, the police, were of course able to call off the murder hunt and set to work on clearing up the loose ends. Dacre had a flat in London, and when it was searched some interesting information came to light. He had kept a diary of sorts, which was locked away in a drawer in his desk. In his notebook was the record of the killing of no fewer than twelve women, all of them prostitutes — nine in addition to the three with whom he had involved Charles Rowan. The murders had all taken place within the past three years, and each of the women was listed under her first name only, the method of killing being entered briefly as 'strangled', 'smothered', 'stabbed' and once 'gassed'.

There was no elaboration of this last method. Perhaps the victim had been bound and gagged and shut in a car with the engine running and a hosepipe leading in from the exhaust-pipe. Ways of disposal of the bodies were also entered in a similar laconic fashion. Thus: 'buried', 'pit', 'concrete' etc. The last three were: 'Lazar House', 'hump-backed bridge' and 'Charlie's woodshed'.

Detective Sergeant Bilton brought this news to Rowan.

"We thought you ought to be one of the first to know. It'll be in the papers, of course. They'll be bound to make a meal of it."

"So he was a serial killer after all," Rowan said.

"Looks like it. And then I suppose he turned on you because you'd taken his girl from him."

"I didn't take her from him. She had kicked him out before I even knew her."

"Didn't make any difference. He had this grudge against you."

"I suppose he really was insane."

"In my book," Bilton said, "it's called plain bloody evil."

"You'll be hunting for those other bodies, I suppose?"

"Not us. Maybe the Met will. I doubt if they'll find any. Waste of time really."

*

Julia was appalled when she heard the truth about Dacre. "It's hardly possible to believe. And yet I suppose we must. It makes my blood run cold to realise that at one time I was living with a mass murderer. It doesn't bear thinking about."

But she had to think about it, and so did Rowan. It was not something you could stow away at the back of your mind and forget. The one consoling thought was that at least it was over and done with now. Dacre would never be coming back to plague them. Except in nightmares. Except as a phantom haunting them in the dark hours of the night. Except as a ghoulish memory that could never be completely exorcised.

*

When he was discharged from hospital Julia stayed on at Flint Cottage to look after him while he was convalescing. She even brought some of her artist's equipment down from Highgate and did a few paintings of rural scenes. Rowan suggested that now she had become used to the country she might be prepared to give up the London studio and make her stay a permanent one. This suggestion, however, was greeted with utter contempt.

"Not on your life. I'm keeping an account of all the days and weeks I spend here, and I shall expect you to reciprocate with an equivalent length of stay at my place."

"Oh," he said, "don't you think it's a bit of a nonsense all this coming and going between two homes? Why not settle for one? It would be much more sensible, wouldn't it?"

"I entirely agree," she said. "We'll settle for Highgate."

"No. Flint Cottage."

"Toss you for it?"

"Right."

He tossed. She called heads. It came down tails.

"Best of three," she said.

She won the next two.

"Best of five," Rowan said.

He won three-two.

"Okay," she said. "Status quo?"

"Status quo."

*

Ursula rang up. "One of the tabloids would like you to write your story for them. They're thinking of calling it 'The Telephone Killer and I'. What do you say?"

"Nothing doing."

"They're offering pots of money."

"Tell them I only write fiction."

"I told them that."

"What did they say?"

"So do they."

"How much is pots of money?" he asked.

She told him. It was more than he had earned from his last book.

"Tell them I'll think about it."

If you enjoyed *The Telephone Murders*, please share your thoughts on Amazon by leaving a review.

For more free and discounted eBooks every week, sign up to our Endeavour Media newsletter.

Follow us on Twitter and Instagram.

Printed in Great Britain
by Amazon